INEVITABLE AND INVINCIBLE

TOWARDS PEACE, PROSPERITY AND A GOLDEN AGE

by

Dr. Pundit Kamal

RoseDog✲Books

PITTSBURGH, PENNSYLVANIA 15222

ISBN: 978-1-4349-9230-7
Library of Congress Control Number: 2008934162

Printed in the United States of America

First Printing

For more information or to order additional books, please contact:
RoseDog Books
701 Smithfield Street
Pittsburgh, Pennsylvania 15222
U.S.A.
1-800-834-1803
www.rosedogbookstore.com

This book is dedicated to the people of this earth, all of whom are born Universal and Invincible. I hope to awaken and inspire them to create the Inevitable Universal Nation with the force of their peace, love, and compassion.

This is also dedicated to my children and to all the children of this world. They deserve a happy, healthy, prosperous, and enlightened future in a newly created world.

And finally, this is dedicated to the most revered Bhagwan Gurumaharaj, to my respected parents, and my most beloved wife. I thank them for their unselfish and constant love and assistance. I am obliged to them forever.

CONTENTS

TAMSOMAYA...JIOTARGAMIA

LET THE UNIVERSAL TRUTH LEAD US FROM DARKNESS TO ENLIGHTENMENT

PREFACE

I am absolutely convinced that the people of this world are wise, courageous, honest, and industrious. I believe that people from every part of this world have the strength and wisdom to solve their worst problems and to conquer them easily. At present, we all are passing through some very inhuman and severe problems, the solution of which is the creation of the universal nation.

The holy scriptures say that all the gods, goddesses, saints, and prophets have authority over heaven and earth and they can heal and grant happiness, peace, and salvation to all people. They are universally one, united, and the same in spirit; even though they go by different names, they represent the Universal Divine Spirit. This spirit is invincible, and makes the people of the world invincible in their struggle to bring about a golden age for the whole world.

All that glitters is not gold, as the saying goes. This world has not been changed for the better by the rich; but it has certainly been improved by the great philosophers and scientists, who bring to bear their wisdom, hard work, dedication, and unselfish commitment and not by any metaphysical or supernatural powers. Among all the philosophers, Socrates shines like the moon among the stars.

People have been fighting wars for thousands of years and have accomplished nothing except holocaust, genocide, oppression, hunger, poverty, and disease. The conqueror sleeps in sin and brings agony to the conquered. The spoils of war received from the conquered countries are spent in maintaining the military edge, and the people do not see any improvement in their existence. The people of the conquered nations are exploited and face poverty and humiliation. Thus no one benefits; all are losers.

Empire-building is an evil. The First and Second World Wars and the Cold War were fought for this purpose, and trillions of dollars and millions of human lives were wasted as a result. It is insane and foolish to spend so much money and sacrifice so many lives on militarism when the world is experiencing so many economic crises. This money could be spent on health care, food, education, reducing pollution, and much more. This world could become a haven of peace, love, health, literacy, and prosperity.

A leader should not have to be rich financially or need security forces to do his job properly. He must serve his people without expecting anything from them, and with their consent. If he loses the confidence and approval of his people, then he must resign. If, due to his false pride and blindness, he does not resign, then he could be forced to surrender his leadership and would certainly be humiliated.

The leader who can rule his or her soul and honestly serve his or her people with perseverance and altruism can certainly rule the world. It is now time for all the people of this world to rule their souls by adopting the universal virtues of equality, liberty, and fraternity; by doing this, they can rule the world and can easily lead themselves to a state of peace and prosperity. Nothing is impossible, and truly the creation of a universal nation is possible.

The people of this world have been sleeping in the night of nationalism for many centuries. Now they must awaken to the dawn of universalism and rise up and unite to transform all the existing nations to one universal nation and all existing governments to a universal government. All class distinctions would disappear to form Universal Mankind. Thus would we enter into the Utopia of a Golden Age.

It is to be noted that the author began writing this book on September 7, 1988, and finished on August 10, 1990. Thus, various events and incidents cited belong to this time frame.

Dr. Pundit Kamal
October 2007

PROLOGUE

THE SPARROW AND THE OCEAN

Once there was a sparrow who lived in a tree on the edge of the ocean. She laid her eggs in her nest on a branch of the tree. The next day, a big storm came and the ocean boiled up with the winds and swallowed her eggs.

The sparrow flew away, and when the storm was over, she returned and asked the ocean to return her eggs. But the ocean refused to give them back. Then she told the ocean that she would empty out all of its water, and all the fish and other water animals would die.

The ocean replied, "You are so small and weak; how can you empty out my mighty sea? Stop making castles in the air. Go away!"

The sparrow was not daunted. "Although I am small, I have the willpower to recover my eggs. They will be my children, and I love them more than my life. Therefore, I have the invincible will to save my children, and with this power I will drain away all your water."

The little sparrow began to pick up water drop by drop with her beak and deposit it on the land.

Now, some distance away, a prophet was sitting in deep meditation and saw by means of his Divine Light what the sparrow was doing. He appeared in front of the sparrow and asked her why she was taking all the water out of the ocean. She told him her story, and the prophet was incensed that the ocean should have done such an evil thing.

The prophet threatened the ocean: "Unless you return the sparrow's eggs, I will burn away all of your water with my supernatural Divine Fire!"

The ocean returned the sparrow's eggs.

Now, suppose I am like this sparrow, and this whole world is like a huge ocean whose water has become dirty due to the division of the land, nationalism, religionism, racism, militarism, hatred, etc. And it is my invincible will and desire to empty out all this dirty water and retrieve the eggs of Truth, Love, and Hope that have become trapped and buried in it.

And so I start to empty it, a bucket at a time. And the people of the world are watching this on television and want to know what I am doing, so when they come to me and ask, I tell them my story, just like the sparrow. I tell them that once this water is emptied out, it can be replaced with clean water.

The people are thrilled to hear about this, but they say, "You can't possibly do it alone. We will help you!"

It becomes a great humanitarian effort, and more and more people join us to throw out the dirty water, working together in complete harmony and co-operation.

Finally, we get back the eggs and fill up the ocean with clean water. The whole world becomes united, with the help of Truth, Love, and Hope, and we all live happily and harmoniously forever in this ocean of the universal nation.

PART THE FIRST

"SATIA...MAIB...JAYATAY"

"CERTAINLY, THE UNIVERSAL TRUTH ALWAYS WINS."

ONE

THE UNITED UNIVERSAL PEOPLE
THE UNIVERSAL NATION

In this day and age, no one country can be the superpower of the whole world. The nations that were superpowers in the past are no longer so today, and countries that are superpowers today will not be so tomorrow. It is a natural phenomenon that the cycle of power rotates from nation to nation, from era to era, giving an opportunity for every nation to have a turn. We all know that past empires such as the Egyptian, Babylonian, Persian, Ottoman, Indian, Mongolian, and others have faded away. In future, there will be one and only one superpower: the united universal people, and through them, the universal nation.

The emperors of these defunct empires spent the wealth confiscated from those they conquered on maintaining their vast armies, and consequently no one benefited from this wealth. These emperors could not solve the problems of poverty, sickness, and illiteracy of their people because they had to spend all they had on their armies. The Sun King, Louis 14th of France, advised his son, Louis 15th, not to make war, because it is very costly, deadly, and unprofitable.

The people of the world have suffered much from wars. Millions have died, mothers have lost their sons, wives have lost their husbands; it is a matter of great regret that in peace, sons bury their fathers, but in war, fathers bury their sons. Houses have been burned, splendid cities reduced to ashes, and green fields converted to desert. Women have been raped and people made slaves.

Empire-building is an epidemic that still exists in this world where the leaders are educated people. While trillions of dollars are spent on maintaining a military machine, millions of people go to sleep hungry every night, and millions of children become sick and blind and die every year due to malnutrition. Millions of mothers cannot stay at home with their newborn babies but must go to work because of economic reasons. Hundreds of thousands of students drop out of university due to unaffordable expenses, and as many more never have the opportunity even to begin an education.

Empire-building has resulted in "limited wars" such as Korea, Vietnam, Afghanistan, and Cuba, with the same disastrous effects as World Wars I and II. The superpowers and many other nations are facing foreign debt, inflation, and financial deficits. As the insect eats the wood slowly and steadily and at last destroys it, so this empire-building is eating the people slowly and steadily and will ultimately destroy them by creating World War III and a nuclear holocaust. This final conflict will be as dark as night, as powerful as an earthquake, as deadly as poison, resulting in death for us all.

To avoid this horrific outcome, all the leaders must meet together in a universal summit and must give up their desires for nationalism and empire-building and instead plan the creation of a universal government. How this could be done is described thoroughly in the chapters following.

And the heads of all the nations should go to the graves of the soldiers who have died in past wars and express their gratitude. If they truly want to avoid more of these graves in the future, if they truly have love for human life, then they must swear by everything sacred to them that they will do their best to create a new order in the world. They must struggle until their last breath to create the universal nation and universal government. Otherwise they are the enemies of mankind and will not be able to guide the people of the world towards unity, peace, and prosperity. In this case, the people have the right to protect themselves and to replace these heads of government with new, enlightened leaders.

Leaders should benefit the people, not the other way around. They must be like a lamp that burns itself to enlighten the people. They must be shining examples. When the world is going through the crisis of alcoholism, then it is not right for a leader to be drinking alcohol; when this stone age is passing through the disaster of divorce, it is not right for a leader to be divorced. There is a saying: *"Yatha Raja, Tatha Praja."* It means that people work and live according to how their king lives and works, and they follow their king in thoughts, principles, character, and morality. In other words, people are reflections of their leaders. If a leader cannot live an exemplary life, then he must renounce leadership and find another profession.

Those emperors of vast lands who ruled over many countries by the sword created hell for themselves. There is no poet who sings in their appreciation, no carefully tended grave to remind us of them. They persecuted hundreds of thousands of people in the name of this or that religion and tried to change the languages, cultures, religions, and traditions of those they conquered. But due to natural processes, those dominated nations are free today. Similarly, today, those who are trying to dominate weaker nations with the force of their mighty armies will ultimately fail.

Mahatma Gandhi was a living example of a true leader. He led a life of simplicity, renunciation, morality, truth, and meditation. He sacrificed everything for the people of his country, and never accepted any special position or rank. Millions of Indians and foreigners followed him and his teachings.

Gandhi found out that many poor people had no clothes to wear, so he decided not to wear clothes—just a minimal covering for the body. He had only one wooden bowl and wooden spoon for eating, and one pair of shoes that he made with his own hands.

With his principles of peace, love, truth, unity, and non-violence, Gandhi won the hearts of millions of people of Great Britain, having a strong effect on India's later independence. Although he took no rank in the government of India, neither before nor after freedom, still he is known as the Father of India, and many heads of nations go to Gandhi's grave to pay tribute.

Today, Gandhi stands as a holy saint and a true leader. Now is the time for all the leaders of all the nations of the world to follow his principles of love, unity, and non-violence.

Siddhartha Gautama Buddha was a true emperor. He was born into a royal family and was the only prince of Kapilavastu, of the Sakya Republic, Kosala kingdom, in India. He renounced his kingdom and went to the forest to meditate. After twelve years of asceticism and penances, he attained Nirvana. Due to his true knowledge of the Divine Light, he was worshipped by millions of people, even by many emperors and kings. He is still revered and worshipped by millions of Buddhists, and in doing so they attain enlightenment, Nirvana, peace, prosperity, health, and happiness, and all their wishes are granted.

In common with Buddhism is another religion in India known as Jainism. The name of their god is Bhagwan Mahavir. His fundamental teachings are that only by renouncing worldly life can one attain the enlightenment that would end the eternal round of incarnations. Of the six great vows that are central to Jainist belief, the most important is that of non-violence. The other five are: renunciation, right faith, right conduct, austerity, and knowledge.

Due to their belief in non-violence, the Jains are vegetarians, do not wear shoes—to avoid stepping on and killing insects—, and wear masks so that they will not kill insects by inhaling them. Due to renunciation, many of them stay naked. It is said that Mahatma Gandhi learned the lesson of non-violence and renunciation from this faith. By worshipping Bhagwan Mahavir, people achieve Nirvana and experience peace, prosperity, health, and happiness.

Emperor Ashoka, of the vast empire of India, fought the war of Kalinga, in which 150,000 soldiers were killed. Seeing the death of so many soldiers, his heart was moved, and he took an oath to fight no more wars. He became a disciple of Gautama Buddha.

He became a monk and gave up his throne of gold and diamonds and his clothes of gold, silver, and silk. He gave up smoking, hunting, and sex. He gave up using force to rule over his vast empire, yet ruled for years in peace, love, forgiveness, and non-violence.

Ashoka said, "He who can rule over his own soul can rule over this whole world without any kind of force, police or military."

The god Krishna was born in a jail cell, where his parents were imprisoned by his own maternal uncle King Kansa. From his childhood, Krishna started to do miracles. According to the ancient legend, he lifted up the mountain Gobhardan Parvat on his baby finger; he cured people suffering from all kinds of chronic diseases; he stopped the shining of the sun; he lifted up the whole city of Mathura and replaced it with all her inhabitants in the Indian Ocean and called it Dwarkadeesh, the City of Gold; he resurrected the dead; and he won the great battle of Mahabharata without using any weapons. When the devil king Kansa sent many demons to kill him, Krishna killed them all and gave them all the gift of salvation, thus breaking the pride of this king.

On the battlefield, Krishna revealed the Holy Scripture Gita to his warrior-devotee Arjuna, which has become immortalized in the *Bhagavad-Gita*. This holy scripture teaches equality of all the creatures—humans, insects, birds, fish, and so on. Humans are to be seen as equal despite their differences in colour, nationality, culture, religion, languages, class, and gender. The one and only universal spirit exists in all; and the person who truly understands this is sinless and wise, and the universal truth lives in him or her. The person who treats equally happiness and suffering, respect and disrespect, ugliness and beauty, enemy and friend, rich and poor, and renounces all his/her mundane desires without attachment, is known to be wise.

The Infinite Universality of the Infinite Divine Human Being (the God Krishna) is worshipped by millions of Hindus, and by doing so they attain knowledge, enlightenment, salvation, peace, prosperity, health, and happiness; and all their wishes are granted.

In Punjab, India, there appeared ten great and holy gurus of the Sikhs. These gurus spoke and fought against injustice, unfairness, oppression, foreign rule, and barbarism. Their fifth guru, Guru Arjun Dev Ji, was fried alive in the hot sands; their ninth guru, Guru Tegh Bahadur Ji, was beheaded. And their tenth guru, Guru Govind Singh Ji, fought against suppression and subjugation his whole life. In the end, he gave away his life for the cause of goodness and humanity, and his two teenage sons were buried alive in brick walls by the enemy. As well, thousands of other Sikhs were beheaded, tortured, and burned alive, a sacrifice unparalleled in the medieval history of India.

These ten gurus, from Guru Nanak Dev Ji to Guru Govind Singh Ji Maharaj, were believed to be incarnations of God himself. They all performed thousands of miracles during their lives, such as curing the lame, deaf, and blind, and resurrecting the dead. Their stories are quite wonderful.

All these gurus revealed and recited the Holy Scripture Sri Guru Granth Sahib, which proclaims that God is One, eternal, invincible, and immortal. He never dies, is never born—he is self-created. He is omnipresent, omnipotent, and omniscient. Their great and holy commandment is to worship God by reciting his name at all times, and to honour Him by your body, mind, soul, thoughts, and actions. The Sikhs—as well as all the people of this earth—will sacrifice their lives for the cause of humanity, peace, health, and harmony.

From childhood, the Holy prophet Mohammed was a sincere devotee of Holy Allah, worshipping Him constantly with every breath. By the mercy of Allah, the Holy Koran was revealed to him. He followed this scripture his whole life and preached it to his disciples.

The teachings of the Koran are to have unshakeable faith in Allah, never to accept the superiority of any man, to be honest and non-judgmental, give to the poor, and bow completely to the will of Allah. Mohammed alone began the great deed of worshipping Allah, and the millions of people who do so find peace, salvation, happiness, and health.

Holy Jesus Christ lived among the poor, loved them, listened to their problems, and cured their diseases. He cured the lame, the deaf and dumb; he resurrected the dead. He calmed the storm, materialized bread and fish to feed thousands of his hungry followers, and converted water to wine. He empowered them with spiritual strength.

Jesus did not rule over nations; he did not live an extravagant life. Due to his power of holiness, renunciation, righteousness, devotion, love, compassion, and forgiveness, he is loved, revered, and worshipped as the Holy Son of God by millions of people of this world. His disciples follow his commandments of love, non-judging, and forgiveness and find peace, health, and happiness.

The Holy prophet Moses was a true political, spiritual, and social leader of his people. He renounced the throne of Egypt and sacrificed his princely life for the welfare of his people. He was sent into exile by the pharaoh of Egypt. In exile, he heard the voice of God, who bestowed upon him spiritual powers. He came back to Egypt and freed all the Jews from the cruel hands of the pharaoh by parting the Red Sea so that they could escape. At last he ascended to Heaven and left us his Ten Commandments.

Judaism is one of the oldest religions of this world. The Jews had been dispersed from era to era, but miraculously came back again as prophesied by their prophets and rebuilt their nation. They had been victims of extreme prejudice, discrimination, hatred, genocide, and oppression; but with their wisdom, tolerance, patience, unceasing and firm faith, hard work, and perseverance, they have successfully survived. The whole world has benefited from their inventions and scientific discoveries, their achievements in all of the arts, and their unselfish service in many other fields.

When Christians create pictures and statues of Jesus Christ or Mother Mary, or of the many saints and angels of God, or of the cross, it is not idol worship. When Buddhists create pictures and statues of Buddha and worship him as their supreme God, the incarnation of Vishnu himself, then it is not the pagan worship of idols. Similarly, when Hindus create pictures and statues of their supreme gods and goddesses, it is not pagan idol worship. These are some of the real, true, and honest ways to worship their gods and goddesses according to their faith, and they have been doing this since the beginning of this world and will continue to do so.

Some of the greatest philosophers in the history of the world, such as Socrates, Plato, and Aristotle, have taught that all beings are equal, regardless of differences in physical characteristics, races, cultures, languages, and beliefs. They all have the one and only Universal God within them. The great scientist Einstein, who was also a philosopher, and Pundit Nehru, the first prime minister of free India, both believed in the universalization and globalization of the world and the creation of a universal nation. They claimed to be citizens of the world. If all leaders would follow the examples of the above-mentioned philosophers and spiritual teachers, and renounce the false goal of empire building, our world would be a heaven and a haven for all.

Two

Universal Oneness

All the different nations are just various sections of the holy motherland earth. The countries are formed of the people who live in them; nations are for the people, not the other way around.

The division of the motherland into nations is a crime and has been the reason for wars from time immemorial. If we wish to banish all wars, then we must struggle to destroy these illusive boundaries within our earth. People of different nations are ready to sacrifice their lives, wealth, and sons for the safety and security of their countries. But this kind of false concentration and useless sacrifice has failed to solve their economic, political, social, religious, and territorial problems. If all these people of all these nations were to put the same concentration and energy into the creation of one true universal nation, all of the problems could be solved.

One true universal nation would mean the obliteration of discrimination and the annihilation of war forever. All the peoples of the world would be united and a universal government could be formed.

If a mother has five sons, and these sons do not live in harmony, as one family, then the mother is always unhappy. Her sadness, family division, and family conflict can cause the deterioration of the family. Similarly, all the people of the world are the sons and daughters of holy mother earth. All her sons and daughters are not living together as one universal family, but are living in different nations, always in conflict among themselves. Because of this, the sacred mother is not happy. The downfall of all these separate families could occur through a nuclear holocaust, resulting in complete destruction of nations and peoples.

Thus, if people want to continue to live and to see their children live and prosper in the future, they must replace the illusive nations and nationalism, their true enemies, with a universal nation filled with true patriotism and universalism.

For many centuries, the earth has been divided into many nations. People of large nations but small populations are enjoying prosperity, but those of small countries with large populations are suffering congestion and poverty. The solution of these problems is the creation of the universal nation, which is feasible. All the people would be free to live and work in any part of the world, thus evening out the distribution of populations.

In 1492, Christopher Columbus explored America. The Spanish people discovered Mexico. In 1497, Vasco da Gama discovered India. The Dutch discovered Indonesia, and the British explored Japan. These were big achievements in those ancient times.

But now, transportation and communications are very advanced. What is happening in one corner of the world can be seen on television on the other side of the world. In the West, one can talk with one's relative from the Far East on the telephone. By airplane, one can travel around the world in a few hours. These wonders of science have converted the vast world to a small village. It would be very easy to unite the people of the earth and create one universal nation.

In the past, most of the people were not educated; but today, education is widespread and available to almost everybody. Through education, people are taught to know the value of peace, unity, love, respect, and non-violence. This, too, would facilitate the formation of a universal government.

All the wars of the ancient ages and the First and Second World Wars were the result of a lack of education. But at the present time, the world is full of teachers who have produced millions of educated people. Knowledge is power. Literate people must use this power to put a stop to war forever and strive for the creation of a universal nation. In this way, they would be giving their sincere and fruitful service to all people and to future generations.

To administer this world with one universal government would be very easy. One can see how some superpowers are controlling many nations of the world by means of their military and economic resources. They are doing this for their own political and economic benefit. On the other hand, the universal government would be very fair and honest, because no one group within the whole would benefit—the whole world would benefit equally.

No People Are Foreign

All the peoples of all the different nations belong to one and only one universal family—the family of mankind. According to all the holy scriptures of all the religions of the world, all people are brothers and sisters, having been created by the Holy Father (or Supreme Consciousness). We are all breathing the same air, drinking the same water, enjoying the same sunlight, eating the same products of Mother Earth. We all are born with the same Divine Light and, at the end of life's long journey, will face the same death. Therefore I can safely write that all people are essentially the same; no people are foreign.

Our bodies are made up of air, water, earth, and the same chemical elements as the sun, moon, and stars! We all have the same red blood flowing in our veins; we have the same respiratory, digestive, and disposal systems; the compositions of eyes, ears, noses, mouths, hands, arms, legs, feet, stomachs, and brains are the same for all of us. The tongue of every body has the same quality of taste, the mouth eats in the same way, the eye sees in the same way, the nose has the same quality of breathing, the feet walk the same way. The mind has the same ability to think, remember, and imagine. The heart has the same ability to love.

All people are the same; no one is foreign.

Oneness in Multiplicity

Due to our ignorance, people may appear different. We see all different kinds of political, religious, social, cultural, linguistic, and economic systems, but basically all are one. Divisiveness is ignorance; oneness is true knowledge. Divisiveness creates discrimination, war, and poverty; oneness opens the doors of peace, love, unity, and prosperity. Oneness is the door to heaven and salvation. All our problems of militarism, war, terrorism, nationalism, apartheid, and poverty are due to divisiveness. Divisiveness is a disease of the heart, and we can kill this disease with the medicine of oneness.

In different parts of the world, people worship different kinds of gods and read different kinds of holy scriptures. But there is one and only one infinite and sacred power, which exists in and controls everything—even the infinite number of planets rotating in space. At different times, holy saints have appeared who have given this power different names, due to their different languages, and have written different holy scriptures based on their experiences and understanding. They have different religious festivals and celebrations. But the central idea is one and the same. They are all teaching the same lesson of meditation, devotion, forgiveness, peace, love, respect, kindness, sincerity, and sacrifice. Thus, there is oneness in multiplicity.

There is only one sun; yet it is called by many names, due to the different languages. But these different names do not mean that there are many suns. Similarly, the One Power is known by many names, e.g. Holy Divine Light, Vishnu, Shiva, Brahma, Holy Guru, God, Allah, Supreme Being, etc. Consequently, I can say that all people are worshipping the One Holy Power. Thus, there is oneness in multiplicity.

The different religions are different methods to worship the One Universal Divine Power. This power is self-created. It is above anger, greed, ignorance, hatred, discrimination, jealousy, and desires. It does everything directly and indirectly, with involvement and without involvement. It is at the same time very near to us and very far away. It is in us and outside of us. It is everywhere and nowhere. Thus, there is oneness in multiplicity.

In the Hindu culture, a couple marries in a temple; a Muslim couple marries in a mosque; a Christian couple marries in a church; a Sikh couple marries in a gurudwara. Marriages take place in different ceremonies and traditions, depending on the culture. But the goal of marriage is the same: to unify the husband and wife spiritually so that they can share each other's happiness and suffering throughout their lifelong journey. In conclusion, I can say that although there are various cultures, still they are all one in their real purpose, goal, and central idea.

All over the world, people are speaking different languages, but they can be translated into each other easily. The central idea of all the languages is to express ideas between and among people. These languages appear different, due to the different pronunciations, alphabets, and words. But all languages have the same goal. Although people might seem different due to their different appearances and languages, basically they are the same.

All peoples of different nations unfurl their national flags in their various cities and fly them high in the sky. These flags may look different in colour, shape, and design, but their aim is one and the same: to display and confirm the nation's pride. They are symbols of sacrifice, service, patriotism, and unity. There are different political systems, such as communism, democracy, dictatorship, theocracy, etc., and different economic systems, such as socialism and capitalism. But again, their goals are the same: to make it possible for their people to live together in peace, harmony, and prosperity. There is oneness in multiplicity.

The universal language understood by everyone everywhere is mathematics. Percentage is always calculated the same way. The area of a right-angled triangle is always the base times the altitude divided by two, and the area of a square is side times side. The Pythagorean Theorem states that the square of the hypotenuse of a right-angled triangle equals the sum of the squares of the other two sides, written in shorthand the world around: $c^2 = a^2 + b^2$. There are universal constants such as π (3.1416...) and $\Box$ (1.618...) that are the same wherever you go. The laws of physics and chemistry do not change from country to country! And so on. Oneness in multiplicity.

The Universal Human Family

There is not a single human being, male or female, young or old, who does not live in the Ocean of Universal Energy. We are all brothers and sisters living in one and only one universal house of the universal nation. We must all make sacrifices to protect this universal human family.

All the peoples of the numerous nations of the world are facing many kinds of problems. These problems do not belong to the people of any one country; they belong to all. Each country tries to solve them, but they continually fail. We must unite in order to solve them.

Children of one country are the same as the children of any other country. They are innocent and happy; they do not know about discrimination, lying, cheating, revenge, manipulation, and enmity. They are the reflection of the Holy Father. They reduce our fatigue and mental pressures. They give us happiness.

Children are pure in their hearts and souls; they are the flowers of the universal garden. We of the universal human family are the gardeners, and we must serve them best so that they will not wither. We must protect them from nuclear holocaust, from wars, from a polluted environment. To love and care for children is to love and care for the universal nation.

As our problems become universal, so must we also become universal. As members of the universal human family, we will solve all our problems, and will begin finally to live in a golden age of peace, prosperity, unity, and humanity.

Universal Oneness

We are one in the bond of Universal Oneness
We are one in the One Universal Life
We are one in the One Universal Nation
We are one in the One Universal Family

We are one in the bond of Universal Oneness
We must start a universal revolution for Universal Oneness
We must struggle and sacrifice for Universal Oneness
We must dedicate ourselves and work for Universal Oneness

We are one in the bond of Universal Oneness
We are one in the one universal sun,

We are one in the one universal sky,
We are one in the one universal air.

We are one in the bond of Universal Oneness.
While others sleep,
We will work for Universal Oneness;
When others flee,
We will fight for Universal Oneness.

We are one in the bond of Universal Oneness
We are one in the one Universal Motherland
We are one in the one Universal Soul
We are one in the one Universal Water.

We are one in the bond of Universal Oneness.
Universal Oneness is the bond of universal health and universal wealth.
Universal Oneness is the bond of universal peace and universal literacy.
Universal Oneness is the bond of universal liberty and universal life.
Universal Oneness is the bond of universal nation and universal government.

We are one in the bond of Universal Oneness.
As long as the sun shines,
We will struggle for Universal Oneness.
As long as the wind blows,
We will sacrifice for Universal Oneness.
As long as we have lives,
We will dedicate ourselves to Universal Oneness.

THREE

DISASTERS OF CLASS STRUGGLE

Class struggle has played a very important role in all the ancient wars, rebellions, terrorism, and religious persecutions. Many classes exist in this age of darkness, such as those based on skin colour, or religion, or level of economic success. If we could eliminate classes, we could annihilate many of society's present and future problems.

Class distinctions such as those based on skin pigmentation have been created by nature and have been in this world since the beginning. There are national and continental classes such as Canadians, British, French, Indians, Chinese, Japanese, Israelis, Arabs, Africans, etc.

Those people who lived on the banks of the river Sindhu in India (now in Pakistan) were called Hindus, 2,600 years before the Holy Buddha appeared in Kapilavastu. Those who followed his teachings became known as Buddhists. The holy prophet Mohammed appeared in Saudi Arabia approximately 1,368 years ago, and those people who followed him began to worship Holy Allah; their religion became known as Islam. The Holy Prophet Guru Nanak appeared in Punjab in India, about 520 years ago, and his disciples are known as Sikhs. The Jewish people worship God according to the Ten Commandments; the followers of Jesus are known as Christians, the major divisions being Catholics and

Protestants. Many religions have sub-religions, or sects, and their beliefs vary slightly from the original faith.

Before the Hindus existed, according to the holy scripture *Srimad Bhagavatam*, the people of India were known as *Sanatans*, which means "as old as the beginning of the universe and as new as today." This is why millions of Hindus still call themselves Sanatans and call their religion Sanatan Dharam. According to the legend of thousands of years ago, there was an emperor named Arya Vrat who ruled over most of the world of that time; due to him, India was once known as Arya Vrat. (Before this, India used to be known as Ikshvaku.) During the reign of this emperor, millions of people, many of whom were Sanatans, became Aryans, and their holy scriptures were called "Vedas."

Hundreds of years after the death of Emperor Arya Vrat, many people of India renounced their Aryan status and went back to being Sanatans. But there are still hundreds of thousands of Aryans living in India, and their religion is known as Arya Smaj (*smaj* means society). This Arya Smaj was founded by the great saint Swami Dayanand Saraswati. He was not only a saint, he was a great educationist. Today, there are hundreds of schools and colleges by his name spread across India.

Then, Emperor Bharat ruled over vast India, and the name of India was again changed, this time to Bharat. This is why India is still known as Bharat in the official language of India.

In the thirteenth century, King Qutab-ud-Din Aibak of Turkey attacked India and subjugated the northwest territories. He made New Delhi his capital. He named his conquered territories Hindustan, and her people were called Hindus.

In the Middle East, there were the gods Baal, Manish, and Anu, and there was the prophet Zarathustra of Persia (now Iran). The people of Babylon (now Iraq) used to worship the god Bail Marduk. History reveals that the people of Egypt once used to worship the sun as a god; the temple of Rameses still stands in Egypt. In South America, as well, there were sun worshippers. Many religions exist and have existed for centuries; but nowadays there are a few religions that claim the majority of the world's population: Christianity, Judaism, Buddhism, Islam, and Hinduism.

In the seventeenth century, the great British philosopher John Locke championed the rights of the people. In his two books, *Human Understanding* and *Two Treatises on Government*, he defended the rights of equality, liberty, life, property, and brotherhood. The glorious revolution of England in 1688 vindicated Locke, and England became democratic. Thus, a new class came into existence: democrats.

Communism was created by the great Karl Marx, who wrote *The Communist Manifesto* and *Das Kapital*. This political and economic system was first put into action by Lenin in Russia in 1917, by means of a revolution. Those who follow it are known as communists. Two other classes are socialists and capitalists.

After the emergence of democracy and communism, many kings and queens disappeared, and nowadays only a few still exist, e.g. the Queen of England and the kings of Jordan, Saudi Arabia, Nepal, etc.

Although all these classes seem different in their philosophies, their *central idea* is the same; they serve the same purpose.

Everyone loves his or her own class, having been born into it. That does not mean, however, that to love one class one must hate all others. Hating all the other classes leads to class struggle—which leads to catastrophe. We must instead follow the principle of *live and let live*.

This world is like an ocean, with tides that rise and fall; the ocean is not affected by these tides. Similarly, the tides of classes rise in the ocean of mankind, and these classes have no effect on mankind as a whole. As the ancient classes do not exist in the present, similarly present classes will not exist in the future.

All people of all classes should realize that they all belong to the one Universal Family and their government is the one Universal Government. The true family of universality will destroy all class struggle and class distinctions and will unite all peoples of all nations. This in turn will prevent the future catastrophes of war, famine, pollution, homelessness, and so on.

There are many national and religious leaders who advocate violence, either due to nationalism, inspired by patriotism; or due to their religious beliefs, inspired by their religious scriptures. Believe it or not, there are holy scriptures that encourage the use of violence in the name of religion! We absolutely must not commit violence as suggested in these scriptures. We can choose to follow their good, positive teachings and ignore the negative.

"My class is better than yours. I am proud of my class. I was born in my class and I will die for it. All people must be converted to my class by force or peacefully. All people of my class must be united and must always be stronger and mightier so as to crush other classes. The people of my class must be richer than the others."

This kind of ignorance leads to class struggle. It makes people stupid and destroys the true knowledge of the soul. It leads to discrimination, jealousy, and, in the end, to untimely death—it is the road to Hell. There are many disasters of class struggle and some of them are described below.

Human Persecution

Many strong kings and emperors were controlled by the evil of class struggle. Due to this, millions of innocent men, women, and children suffered. They dominated people of other nations and destroyed their languages, religions, cultures, and basic human rights. In some cases they made slaves of defeated peoples. They ruled over the people with cruel and inhuman laws. They took all the natural resources from their nations.

But all those dictators who persecuted innocent people created hell for themselves and lost the treasures and happiness of their own spirit.

Wars

Nations have been fighting wars due to class struggle for many centuries. England vs. France; Soviet Union vs. France; France vs. Germany; Soviet Union vs. Mongolia and Eastern Europe; Iran vs. Iraq; India vs. Pakistan; South Korea vs. North Korea; the list goes on and on. An even greater list is the civil wars within all the countries, which many times served to change the class structure of the countries involved. Millions of people died or were maimed for life. If we want to stop wars, we must destroy the class struggle forever.

Subjugation

Different nations have been subjugated by stronger empires for many centuries. The British Empire dominated Canada, Egypt, India, Burma, various parts of Africa, Australia, and so on. Remnants of British rule remain in those areas even today. The French Empire took over Vietnam, Laos, Cambodia, Madagascar, Algeria, Morocco, and parts of Africa. The Ottoman Empire of Turkey, the Soviet Union, Portugal, Germany…the list of conquerors goes on.

William Shakespeare wrote, "Uneasy lies the head that wears a crown." The leaders of those empires gained very little from their victories and lost their peace of mind. They needed to maintain vast armies in order to stay on top. Many of the subjugated countries were prevented from further economic development and faced poverty, disease, and illiteracy.

It is the first and foremost duty of all peoples of all nations to resist and put a stop to all forms of domination, so that in future all can live in universal peace, freedom, prosperity, literacy, and good health. This is only possible under the creation of a universal government, which will unify all peoples of all nations.

Civil War

Civil war also is the result of class struggle. Spain, the U.S.A., India, and many other nations have suffered from this evil. If class distinctions were nonexistent and all people treated each other with respect and kindness, civil war would be unnecessary. Such a condition would exist if all the peoples of all nations were to unite under the umbrella of a universal nation.

Guerrilla Warfare

This is happening in many places in the world today, again due to class struggles. This is carried out by small bands of individuals who are fighting for their ideals, sometimes against the government of their country. Guerrillas are usually from poor and weak nations, and have no money to buy weapons; but often they have support from stronger nations that will supply them with sophisticated weapons, food, and clothing, hoping to help undermine the government of that country.

As usual, it is the innocent civilians that suffer. Children have been kidnapped by guerrillas and terrorists and trained to fight. Others have been killed. Without class distinctions, without cruel domination, there would be no guerrillas.

Militarism

The arms race and the cold war are the result of class struggle. People of one class want to destroy people of another class; people of one class believe theirs is better, more successful, holier, than all others. Thus it has always been.

But this is wrong, ignorant thinking. After all, when a person is born into a particular class, he or she has no understanding of any other class. Since childhood, he has heard from his parents, religious and political leaders, and teachers that his class is the best. These leaders and teachers are sowing the seeds of hatred and militarism.

Nowadays, billions of dollars are being spent all over the world on militarism. Due to this, governments are unable to spend their money on food, clothing, medical aid, and education. Millions are left illiterate, hungry, and sick. Millions live in fear of future wars and nuclear annihilation.

It is the first and foremost duty of the leaders of all nations to destroy the evil of class struggle and work instead for the creation of a universal nation and a universal government. As water always flows from above to below, so also do evil and goodness. Leaders are at the top of the hierarchy, and their attitudes will flow down to the people. If leaders everywhere will fill up their souls with goodness, then it will flow down and terrorism and militarism will disappear.

Universal Apartheid

This is another kind of class division, best known in South Africa. But class struggle has created a sort of universal apartheid, divid-

23

ing this earth by the false and narrow walls of various kinds in different nations. It is another way of describing the class struggle that we have been discussing, and is again based on the illusive distinctions of religion, politics, skin colour, and so on.

The solution to universal apartheid is to become one true and fruitful universal family. This will lead to a universal nation and universal government.

Division of Territories
Due to internal class struggle and external interference, blood brothers are forced to kill each other. North Korea fought South Korea; North Vietnam fought South Vietnam; India and Pakistan became divided; Germany was partitioned into East and West. This is unjust and cruel, and a true universal government would automatically unite these brothers again.

Religious Killing
Some people have been killing on the cause of this and that religion, God, Goddess, holyman, holy scripture etc. since the beginning of this world. Religious Killing is banned all over this world and it is punishable by capital punishment.

Conclusion
In the past and at the present time, people have suffered and do suffer in many ways from class struggle and class distinctions. If in the future they want to live a life of peace, prosperity, good health, and literacy, and want to protect their children from a nuclear holocaust, then they must be ready to dedicate themselves to the struggle for a universal nation.

FOUR

INEVITABLE AND INVINCIBLE

The present political systems have failed to solve all the problems that exist in all the nations: future global nuclear war, militarism, terrorism, poverty, disease, and pollution. It is the first and foremost duty of all the people of this world to unite and invent a new political system.

Nature always sends great souls full of truth, wisdom, and enlightenment who can enlighten and strengthen us so that we can solve our problems. Such great souls as Locke, Voltaire, Rousseau, Mahatma Gandhi, Lincoln, Marx, and Lenin led the way to wisdom, truth, and enlightenment and helped to abolish monarchy. New political and economic systems of communism, democracy, socialism, and capitalism began to emerge, and millions of people have benefited from these systems. Similarly, the present systems can be replaced by newer, better ones.

Enlightened teachers—indeed, all people—can find the ways and means of avoiding all our present and future disasters by forming a universal family and a universal government. The resulting good fortune would not be a matter of divinity or luck, but the result of our own actions—our hard work, dedication, and struggle.

Nothing happens without struggle. Nothing is solved without struggle. The earth produces as a result of the struggles of the farmer. The machine turns out parts due to the struggles of the worker. Teachers teach, students learn, patients recover from illness, children are born and raised, wars are won—always with a struggle.

Therefore, my Dear Universal People, stand up and fight your true enemies: nationalism, militarism, religionism, war, poverty, inflation, sickness, and illiteracy. You must not rest until they are crushed all the way to their roots.

There are examples from the past.[1]

The people of England under the leadership of the great leader Oliver Cromwell struggled and sacrificed their lives for the destruction of monarchism and the creation of democracy. In 1646, King Charles I and his army surrendered. In 1649, this king was beheaded, and his army could not protect him. At last, in 1688, democracy came to England, and the monarchy became the ceremonial leader or figurehead of the nation. Due to democracy, slavery disappeared from England, and her people won equal rights in speech, education, religion, politics, and economics. Democracy became the major reason for the prosperity and development of the people of England, and also of many others in nations that became democratic by following England's example.

Voltaire and Baron Montesquieu of France visited England. They were very much impressed with the democratic system they observed there. They were moved by the quality of liberty, life, fraternity, and freedom of expression. They went back to France and began to preach democracy. The King of France, who was an absolute monarch, became apprehensive and sent Voltaire into exile. There, Voltaire wrote a book on democracy. Jean-Jacques Rousseau also wrote a book on democracy and inspired the people of France to struggle to achieve it.

Later, Georges Jacques Danton played an important part in the early years of the French Revolution, inspiring the people to struggle against monarchism. Many philosophers, thinkers, and idealists played a part in this great revolution. King Louis XVI ordered his army to fire on the revolutionaries, but they refused to

---

[1] This is a broad overview.

shoot because they were satisfied that the people were right and the king was wrong.

The King of Austria, a friend of Louis XVI, sent his soldiers to help out, but the people of France defeated all of them. Finally, King Louis was taken by the people and sent to prison and later executed. While in jail, King Louis came to the conclusion that it was not the people of France who had destroyed him and his kingdom, but the books of Voltaire and Rousseau.

When democracy came to France, it affected the whole world, especially Eastern and Western Europe. Slowly, over time, monarchies were overthrown, one country at a time. The people with their power of unity, struggle, and sacrifice succeeded in overthrowing the unsuccessful old political systems and in ushering in the formation of new, successful systems of democracy and communism.

The United States of America was at one time a British colony. Its people wanted their freedom from Great Britain, and fought against the British forces under the leadership of the great and brilliant George Washington. In 1789, the future U.S.A. became a republic with Washington as her first president.

The great genius Abraham Lincoln was born of a poor family. The story goes that since Lincoln had no money to buy books, he borrowed a book from his friend. It rained all night and some dampness came into the house and ruined the book. His friend's father asked him to pay for the book, but Lincoln had no money. He had to work many weeks on his farm to pay for that book.

Due to his honesty, hard work, perseverance, dedication, and struggle, Lincoln became a lawyer, and then became president of the U.S.A. Due to his honesty, he was referred to as "Honest Abe." He was the first great soul to fight against the slavery in the U.S. and free the blacks. It was a great shock to the whole world when he was shot and killed.

Lincoln was not only the greatest president of the U.S.A., but of the whole world. After him, the great Dr. Martin Luther King Jr. followed Gandhi's principle of non-violence and succeeded in attaining perfect freedom for the blacks in the U.S. As well, the great Nelson Mandela followed Gandhi's example and managed to free the blacks of South Africa.

The mighty Czars of Russia ruled over this nation with strong hands and were not ready to renounce their power to her people. But two great political leaders emerged—Vladimir Ilyich Lenin and Leon Trotsky—who urged revolutionary action to remove the Czar and enter a new age of freedom. The people of Russia struggled with firm determination and sacrifice, and Czar Nicholas tried his best to crush them. But again, his soldiers refused to fight; they renounced the Czar and joined the people. The Czar had to take refuge in Holland.

The great soul Lenin guided the people of Russia, and in 1917, Russia became communist. Czarism was not obliterated without pain, but it was finally destroyed by the struggle and revolt of the Russian people.

Therefore, my Dear Universal People, if all of you want a universal nation and a universal government, do not waste any more time. Do not wait for the solution of your problems, but continue working and sacrificing for a better world.

The Moslem leader Jinah received the nation of Islamic Pakistan on August 14, 1947, from the British.

The champion of liberty Mujiber Rahman freed Bangladesh from Pakistan in 1971.

India was subjugated by the British Empire. There were many leaders in India who resisted this domination: Maharana Ranjit Singh of Punjab, Bhagwan Tilak, Pundit Chander Shekhar Azad, Shahid[2] Rajguru, Netaji Subhash Chander Bose, Pundit Nehru, Lala Lajpatrai, Shahid Bhagat Singh, Shahid Sukhdev, the Maharani Zhansi of Zhansi, Sardar Patel, and so on. Finally, Holy Saint Mahatma Gandhi inspired the people of India to struggle for their freedom with the invincible weapons of non-violence, peace, truth, and equality. Hundreds of millions followed this great soul. On August 15, 1947, India became free of British rule.

About Gandhi it was written that coming generations will scarcely believe that a great soul like Mahatma Gandhi ever

---

[2] "Shahid" is a Hindi word that means "martyr."

walked on the face of the earth. It is said that when Gandhi was taken by the British police to the courtroom of the Supreme Court, the judges would stand to pay him respect.

Great souls never die; their death is only physical. Spiritually they are always alive, and they continue to guide us and constantly enlighten the spirits of the leaders of all the governments towards perfection, justice, peace, unity, and harmony. They continue to shine like the sun and help to banish the night of our spiritual ignorance. How they do this is a very mysterious phenomenon, and is understood only by those who meditate and read the holy scriptures and sit in the presence of saints.

Today the people of all nations must believe in the weapons of Mahatma Gandhi: non-violence, love, justice, co-operation, and equality. We must all struggle and sacrifice for the achievement of universal government. Sacrifice does not necessarily mean sacrifice of blood, flesh, and life, but it means sacrifice of nationalism, militarism, religionism, political systems, and economic systems—all of which create inequalities between peoples.

"This is my political system. I will destroy your inferior political system; I will fight any kind of war for the protection of my political system."

"I will spread my political system/religious beliefs/economic system everywhere, in every nation of the world."

"My economic system is more productive than yours. I will destroy your economic system in every nation."

Does any of this sound familiar? It is nothing new; it has been going on for centuries.

The people of Algeria were subjugated by the vast empire of France. The united people struggled and sacrificed everything for the freedom of their nation. The French government lost thousands of soldiers in their attempt to suppress the Algerians. But the people did not falter in their struggle for independence. France finally gave them their freedom in 1962.

The people of Ghana, under the leadership of Mr. Nkrumah, struggled and fought for their freedom, and the British Empire granted them independence in 1957. Under the brilliant leadership of Mr. Jomo Kenyatta, the people of Kenya rose against the British Empire and won their freedom in 1963.

Vietnam was dominated by France for many years. The great and brave Mr. Ho Chi Minh led his people to resist and defeat the forces of France. Then the U.S. interfered to help France and to establish democracy and destroy communism in Vietnam. But the firm and determined Vietnamese kept on fighting and sacrificing their lives, the lives of their children, and their property. Finally, the armies of the vast and mighty empire of the U.S. pulled out and went home. The people of Vietnam received their independence, and today Vietnam proudly stands free.

Indonesia was subjugated by the Netherlands. The people of Indonesia fought under the leadership of Mr. Achmad Sukarno against the Dutch. As a result of their struggle and sacrifice, they won their freedom at the end of 1949, and Mr. Sukarno became the first president of the free nation.

Under the leadership of Dr. Sun Yat-sen, the people of China destroyed the Manchu Dynasty, and China became a republic, with Sun Yat-sen as president. Later, in 1949, China was declared the People's Republic of China, converted to communism by Chairman Mao Tse-tung (or Mao Zedong).

Considering the above highly simplified bits of history, we can surely see that people were *invincible* in creating *inevitable* forms of democracy or communism almost everywhere. And we can conclude that by universal dedication, determination, struggle, and sacrifice, it is inevitable that eventually there will be a universal nation and universal government. As Emperor Charles I of the British Empire surrendered to the people of England; as Emperor Louis XVI and his armies surrendered to the people of France; and as Czar Nicholas II of the vast empire of Russia surrendered to the people, similarly all governments of all the present nations will eventually surrender to the universal struggle, sacrifice, and fierce determination of the united peoples of all nations of the world; and the soldiers of their armies will act for the people, not against them.

The Universal, Invincible Supreme Power will obliterate all divisions of our holy motherland; it will destroy separateness of all nations and national governments; it will erase all the divisions between peoples; and it will eradicate the nuclear threat that hangs over us at the present time.

The basis of this Power is Universal Truth. This is not an ideology or a fiction. This Truth, the Truth of Enlightenment, has always been accessible in every era and in every part of the world. When it starts to live in the minds of all people, then all will become that truth, just as the magnet makes iron magnetic. When this happens, we can create a universal nation and a universal government.

Truth always prevails. Truth fears no test. Truth fears no sufferings. As air stands alone, giving oxygen to all; as the sun stands alone, giving warmth and light to all; as the ocean stands alone, giving water to all; as the earth stands alone, giving food to all; thus truth stands and shines alone and enlightens all the people of the earth.

Truth is an infinite power; it is as firm as the Himalayas; it is the ruler of the world. It is the true friend and saviour of mankind. It does not follow the mighty governments of the mighty nations and their mighty armies. All these nations must follow the truth and surrender to it. When governments and people move away from truth, they suffer. Today we are suffering for that reason. With the weapon of truth, we must break down the narrow walls of nationalism that has divided all the peoples of the world. The truth will enlighten us and make us invincible.

The creation of a universal government is not new; it is as old as time. Since the beginning of history, there has been universal government from time to time. The Holy Scripture *Shrimadbhagbad*, found in the Hindu religion, was written by the saint Ved Vyas about five thousand years ago. The Holy Guru in this scripture describes main events from the beginning of the world to the end of this world. In the beginning, he says, the world emperor Manu ruled over all the world. After him, world emperors such as Vali, Dhrub, Prahalad, Hirnakashpu, Prithu, Priajit, Ikshvaku, Pundit Ravana, the god Rama, and Yudhishtra, etc., have ruled over the whole world at different periods of ancient history. Emperor Vali and Emperor Pundit Ravana ruled not only the people of this planet, but also the people of many other planets.

In the Hindu religion, the Holy Saint Tulsi Dass wrote the Holy Scripture named *Ramayana*. In it he describes in detail the holy, true, and divine life story of the god Rama. He says that during the reign of Rama, no one was sick, no one was poor, no one was homeless; there was no crime; families were united; and natural disasters such as famine, drought, earthquakes, floods, etc., never took place in any part of the world. All lived in unity, peace, equality, brotherhood, and forgiveness. In his empire, all his subjects enjoyed universal prosperity, health, and literacy. No police were needed, no army was needed; the people were controlled by the natural laws of morality, humanity, and holiness.

Even the animals of the forest renounced their enmity, and the goat and the wolf drank from the same stream. The empire of the god Rama was perfect because *he* was perfect in every aspect of his life. Therefore, a perfect world government is feasible. If we want to have such a perfect world government, then we will have to change ourselves; we will have to strive for perfection in our own lives, each and every one of us. And as we and our leaders become Invincible, a universal nation and a universal government will become Inevitable.

FIVE

UNIVERSAL REVOLUTION

Man is born revolutionary and is destined to revolt from the time he is born until his death. Man revolts for justice, for his rights, for the protection of his family, for the safety of his children, for his honour; and in the end he dies revolting against death.

Nothing constructive seems to happen without productive revolution. Revolution moves events along, causes new developments to happen. The revolts of the people of England, France, and Russia brought in social, political, and economic changes for their nations that spread to other nations as well. When a new revolution takes place, even though at first there is struggle, suffering, and disruption, new and positive developments occur for the people.

Everything happens naturally. Nature sends a great soul according to the necessities of mankind. She creates the atmosphere and circumstances so that the great soul can attain the knowledge necessary and can act according to the needs of the people.

Nature sent the great soul Gorbachev to act for the people of the Soviet Union. His policies of Glasnost and Perestroika started to impress his people and also the people of many other nations. Democratic elections were held in the Soviet Union, and the effects of this were felt in Poland, where elections were held as well. Now elections are being arranged in Hungary, East Germany, and the Czech Republic. Mr. Gorbachev has encouraged the people of these nations and all the other nations of Eastern Europe to create democratic governments.

Waves of freedom began in East Germany. People struggled for that. With the consent of Mr. Gorbachev, the government of East Germany ordered the dismantling of the Berlin Wall so that the people of East Germany could visit the people of West Germany, and vice versa. Many thousands of people from East Germany went to the West, and the people of West Germany welcomed them with open hearts, minds, and souls. So some of them stayed to settle down forever. The leaders and governments of many nations, including the U.S. and England, welcomed the opening of the gates.

For years, nobody could imagine that this could happen. But Mother Nature secretly created the circumstances and atmosphere. Former enemies became friendly and were in agreement over this event. See the invisible and secret miracle of nature, that totalitarian governments are becoming converted to democracy. Mother Nature is invisible and kind and she is everywhere. She will create the atmosphere and circumstances under which all people will become free. Divisions based on political, economic, linguistic, religious, and spiritual boundaries will disappear.

The United States, Canada, England, France, West Germany, India, and many other nations have given their full co-operation, sympathy, and assistance to Mr. Gorbachev and to the people of the Soviet Union, Poland, Hungary, East Germany, and the Czech Republic, and they are ready to give their full support to any other nation of Eastern Europe that might want to bring about democratic changes in her regime.

Destruction of totalitarianism does not necessarily mean the eradication of communism and socialism. The government of any communist country that is shared by the common people or by all the people of that nation is known as a communist government. But a totalitarian government is not shared by all the common people of any nation; therefore, this kind of government can never be known as a communist government. When people elect their own government by secret ballots, then that government is known as a government of the common people.

The women of the world, educated or uneducated, poor or rich, have the virtues, skills, strength, wisdom, perseverance, patience, tolerance, dedication, and commitment to do great and incredible works for the welfare and benefit of humanity. The history of the world is full of the great and talented women who have done great deeds for mankind: Catherine the Great of Russia, Queen Woo of China, Maria Theresa of Austria, Mrs. Indira Gandhi of India, Golda Meir of Israel, Mother Teresa, Susan Anthony of the U.S., Margaret Thatcher of England, and many others. For the creation of the universal nation, all the women of this whole world have to play a major role and fearlessly, with inspiration and boldness, they must join the universal revolution and, by standing shoulder to shoulder with one another, they must continue to struggle for it.

Universal revolution is the revolution of this era, and involves a different sort of revolutionary: universal people. These are not soldiers with guns and bombs. These are people who want freedom and peace instead of war, prosperity instead of poverty, education instead of illiteracy, and a clean environment instead of a polluted one. It is the biggest, strongest, and most powerful revolution of all the revolutions in the history of this earth. It would certainly create the universal nation, which will be the greatest, healthiest, happiest, most peaceful, and most prosperous nation of all.

There are millions of soldiers in the military machines of all the nations of the world. These soldiers do not belong to any leader, nation, or government; they belong to you, to your families. These are your brothers and sisters, mothers, fathers, sons, daughters. They are separated from you: mother is at home, but husband is at the military base; son is at home, but daughter is fighting a war in the desert; father is sick at home, but son is flying in a bomber to attack an enemy target...

This kind of separation is very hurtful. It is inhuman and cruel. A mother who has kept her son or daughter in the womb for nine months, then brought him or her to adulthood with great love, care, and sacrifice, now has to suffer as militarism snatches her child away. Will she ever see her treasure again?

All those soldiers who are dying in various wars are your family members, are the children of your friends. The leaders sit safely in their palaces, mansions, and bunkers while the others do the fighting. If you want to stop this senseless killing, then make a stand. Revolt against war and start a universal revolution for a universal nation and universal government!

The stores are stocked with medicines, but countless people are suffering and dying without medication. The banks are full of money, but many people have no money to build houses and are sleeping on the roads. The markets are full of food, the stores are full of clothing, but many people have no money to buy them. Every nation has at least one university, and some nations have many of them; but thousands of students have no money to attend them, and so they remain illiterate.

Where is all the money going? It is being spent on the military machine, on terrorism, on anti-terrorism. In many parts of the world, the only way to be clothed, fed, and taught (in a limited way) is to join the army or a guerrilla group.

In Sudan alone, one million people died due to hunger when guerrillas cut their food supply lines. In Mozambique, India, Afghanistan, El Salvador, Guatemala, Angola, Sri Lanka, Nicaragua, the Philippines—it goes on and on—hundreds of thousands of people have been killed by guerrillas. They kidnapped young boys to train them for guerrilla warfare. They burned houses, destroyed schools, ruined hospitals, and burned the crops in the fields. To kill civilians—women, children, old people who can't defend themselves—is the most serious crime of all.

And of course the guerrillas themselves lost their lives or became seriously injured. They think they are helping their countrymen, but that is not true. In the end, they are making their nations even poorer. Politics is never won with violence, but with truth, non-violence, peaceful struggle, hard work, co-operation, honesty, and selfless sacrifice. Guerrillas must renounce the methods of violence and force that they have been applying without success for so many years now.

Guerrillas, if you want to help your people and nation, then give up weapons and stop listening to the foreign powers who are destroying all of you and ruining your countries. The end of violence is always defeat and it is the road to poverty. Work instead for a universal nation and a universal government.

The same situation exists with terrorists and hostage-keepers. They, also, are supported and encouraged by foreign nations. They are detaining innocent souls. This does not solve anything. Terrorists and hostage-keepers are creating problems for themselves.

The leaders do not suffer; because of them, billions of dollars are being poured into supporting the military machines, the guerrillas, and the terrorists, all of which are killing us not only physically but spiritually as well. We must not support these misguided leaders. Terrorists must renounce terrorism and protect their own lives and the lives of others. We must all, including the leaders, give our full help and co-operation to running a successful, peaceful, universal revolution for the creation of a universal nation, universal government, and universal family.

This is a dark age in which people are facing many kinds of pressures: financial, psychological, mental, and physical.

The prices of food, clothing, and other consumer goods are going up every month in every nation of the world. When a person goes to rent a house or apartment, he or she often finds that the rent is unaffordable; and once he or she manages to rent a dwelling, every year the rent is increased. The prices of houses just keep rising every year. It has become nearly impossible for middle-class people to buy a house with cash, and so they agree to a mortgage, whose interest rate is very high. For poor people, it is impossible to buy a house under any terms. It seems that half of the money people are earning has to pay for a mortgage or for rent.

Students cannot attend university, because their parents cannot afford the expenses involved. One can imagine the suffering of a young son or daughter who must sit by while his or her friends from rich families continue to study at the universities; and the dismay experienced by the parents who would like to give their child a good start in life. This is suffering caused by financial pressure.

Mental and psychological pressures in the form of fear and worry over nationalism, terrorism, militarism, and religionism are causing diseases of the mind and heart. All the problems of nuclear weapons, the arms race, poverty, sickness, inflation, foreign debt, illiteracy, and so on, weigh down our hearts and minds. Thousands die all the time due to these pressures, and many thousands become sick. To avoid this fear and suffering, many turn to drugs and alcohol. Under the creation of a universal nation, all these problems will be obliterated and these diseases will be destroyed; the psychological pressures will be eradicated.

Physical pressures are experienced by those who are dying to protect this and that religious, political, and economic system. Although death is inevitable, to die for this purpose is a mistake. If we stop these mistakes, then we can prevent the untimely deaths of hundreds of thousands of people.

Hundreds of thousands of children go blind due to malnutrition; if we could feed them properly, this evil would be avoided. Hundreds of thousands of children die every year due to diseases that could be cured or alleviated by medication. Children are orphaned for the same reasons; their parents die from diseases that could have been cured if they had been able to afford the medications.

Universal revolution is indispensable for the life, health, liberty, peace, prosperity, and literacy of the human family. I have described how revolutions in the past, led by such giants as Oliver Cromwell, Georges Jacques Danton, Vladimir Ilyich Lenin, Mahatma Gandhi, and others, have successfully introduced new forms of government to their countries and in most cases increased freedom for their people. Divisions still exist in the world, however, due to the various forms of government and the different religious beliefs. Consequently, it is time for all the peoples of the world to unite, remove the boundaries, and give salvation to all. If we want to accomplish this, we must join this peaceful revolution that is the universal ocean of peace, equality, harmony, and non-violence.

The majority of the people in this world are ignorant, and this is why they are easily misled and overcome by ignorant, self-seek-ing leaders. With universal revolution, education will be available to all and people will not be so easily led astray.

Universal revolution is not against any leader or any government or any nation. It is not against any political, economic, or religious system. Its goal is to *unify* all nations and governments. People will have more opportunities to work and prosper and to live wherever they wish. The only changes brought about by the universal revolution will be at the level of government. Cultures, languages, holy scriptures, traditions—all will remain as they are now.

Natural resources such as oil, gas, diamonds, precious metals, forests, etc., would belong to the people of the area, and their income would be shared. The universal government and respective zonal and provincial governments would charge very low and affordable taxes from their income. No government can ever confiscate these natural resources.

The current leaders will have to give up their seats and give their full co-operation to the creation of the universal nation and universal government. If they can do this, they will be heroes of the universal revolution and their status of leadership will be raised to that of the universal nation. Otherwise, these leaders will be swept away by the infinite universal power, which is like a hurricane or an earthquake: once started, it cannot be stopped. All uncooperative leaders will inevitably wither and die in this blast of energy, and after their death they will be known as traitors.

Those leaders who give their full co-operation will have positions of power in the universal government. The universal nation will also have provincial governments and zonal governments, which I will discuss in a later chapter. Experienced, mature leadership will be needed for these positions.

A new political system is not created by any king, emperor, or national leader. It is created by an invincible great soul full of enlightenment, truth, and wisdom. The enlightened soul comes only after thousands of years, and people continue to follow and live in the creation of this soul until another enlightened soul comes with a creative and beneficial new political system. Such great souls as Locke, Socrates, Rousseau, Marx, Plato, and Mahatma Gandhi came, enlightened the people, and disappeared. Revolutions are created by the books and writings of enlightened souls such as these; the people read the writings and the true and productive revolution starts to live in their hearts and minds. They become revolutionary; the united and committed people start the revolution and succeed in making beneficial changes.

Remember, it is not the leaders, but it is always the people that determine the fate of mankind. The most abundant source of strength lies in the hands of the masses; the enlightened, universal people will always revolt and will find ways to abolish their problems, with every kind of sacrifice, struggle, dedication, and optimism.

There is a choice to be made between development and militarism, because development cannot happen without eliminating militarism. Therefore we must revolt against this evil and work instead for universal government and a universal human family. The age of nationalism, wars, religionism, and militarism has passed; the age of universal peace, equality, brotherhood, prosperity, health, literacy, and unity has begun and will continue on into the future. It is the hope of our children and our children's children, *ad infinitum*.

Because nothing happens without conscious aim, universal truth helps those who help themselves. Thus, we must not wait for any kind of divine intervention to achieve this goal of a universal nation. When we struggle for achievement of a worthwhile goal, the truth will light up our path, helping us in our efforts. The Christian Bible states it very well: "...*for whatsoever a man soweth, that shall he also reap.*"[3] Gal 6:7.

Therefore, Universal People, stand up and sow the seeds of the universal nation and universal government in the universal field of Mother Earth! Irrigate this field with the water of universal revolution. Fence it with your power of unity. Fertilize it with your struggle and sacrifice! Soon it will become a strong, tall,

---

[3] Gal 6:7.

ever-green, universal tree bearing the fruits of your efforts—peace, prosperity, liberty, health, equality, literacy, and harmony for all. And you can reap these fruits with firm determination and non-violence.

The details of how all this is to be done will be covered in the next chapters. One of the new structures would be the Supreme Congress, a universal political party. All must join this party at all levels—family, village, town, city, province, and nation. All will send proposals for the universal nation and universal government to all the leaders and national governments of all the nations of the world.

The people must create an interim universal government based on the universal political system. This government must invite all the governments of all the nations to accept the sovereignty of the universal government, and all the governments must give their consents for the unification of all the nations.

Before the Second World War, many nations put their hopes in the League of Nations, but this body failed to prevent the war. Later, it was replaced by the United Nations.

I respect the United Nations for its efforts towards world peace, but because of the veto powers of Russia, the U.S.A., England, France, and so on, it has become powerless. Although it makes many decisions to promote peace, these decisions are many times cancelled by one of the nations that has veto power. So the UN has become weak. We cannot expect our global problems to be solved by the UN.

If the nations, leaders, and people want to be protected from a third world war, then they must accept the sovereignty of a universal nation and government that would supersede the UN, all nations, and all national governments.

My Revered Universal People! As long as blood flows in our veins, as long as breath flows in our lungs, as long as energy flows in our bodies, let us not rest until we achieve the goal of universal revolution and the unification of all nations!

41

SIX

AWAKEN, UNIVERSAL PEOPLE,
AND
UNITE!

My Revered Universal People! All of you are living in a vast house where four lions are sleeping. These lions are: Nationalism, Religionism, Politicism, and Economicism. Their diet is immense, and they are never satisfied—they eat even when they are asleep!

The Lion of Nationalism has shackled all of you with the chains of national boundaries, so that you cannot easily move from one nation to another. The Lion of Religionism has segregated all of you by the walls of Hinduism, Sikhism, Buddhism, Islam, Taoism, Shintoism, Judaism, Christianity, and so on. The Lion of Politicism has separated all of you by the walls of communism and democracy. The Lion of Economicism has torn your hearts with the piercing nails of socialism and capitalism.

All the lions are eating trillions of dollars in a diet of militarism, and this is destroying all of you by pollution, poverty, sickness, inflation, and foreign debt. These lions have the fierce teeth of atomic, hydrogen, and chemical bombs. If they wake up, they will eat you all with their deadly teeth. Your leaders and governments are unable to see these lions and are too weak to kill them.

We must kill these lions before they wake up.

Therefore, Universal People, you must kill your enemies, the four lions, with the invincible weapon of universal government. The sun of the universal nation has risen. Wake up from your night of ignorance into the light of enlightenment, wake up your leaders, and together work for universal government.

We know that if the ocean is calm it does not mean that the storms will not come. The ocean of this world may be calm now, but it does not mean that the storms of civil wars and World War III will not occur. Coming events cast their shadows before. When clouds gather in the sky, we know it is going to rain. When a civilization falls into the grip of social diseases such as nationalism, racism, religionism, and division, then natural processes will destroy that civilization. It has happened before and it will happen again.

The arms race is the result of nationalism and becomes the cause of economic crisis and in the end causes the proliferation of nuclear weapons. This leads to a polluted environment and the destruction of the ozone layer. The First World War was disastrous, with a huge loss of life, due to the arms race. The Second World War was more disastrous, again due to the arms race. A Third World War could totally obliterate all people, animals, birds, insects—in fact, the whole planet, leaving it uninhabitable for many years to come. I respect and admire all those who gave their lives in both world wars—in all wars, no matter how small.

The arms race is not only just between the superpowers, but it is going on among the smaller nations as well. As leaders have failed to stop the arms race in the past, they will fail to stop it in the future, too, unless there is a Third World War, which will stop everything.

The superpowers in the summit between Mr. Gorbachev and Mr. Reagan have destroyed their many missiles. I appreciate that. But that does not stop the arms race. There is now a new kind of arms race known as Star Wars, which is being developed by both superpowers. This particular arms race is more expensive than all the arms races of previous years. It is the people who will suffer because of this. In both the U.S. and the Soviet Union, people are going without homes, jobs, clothing, food, medical insurance, education…and billions of dollars are being spent on Star Wars.

Leaders claim that Star Wars is an umbrella to protect us from the fatal rays of a nuclear holocaust, but it is not true. The true umbrella to protect us is the universal nation, and it will cost nothing. I am ringing the alarm and asking the people of the world and their leaders to awaken in the light of the sun of the universal nation and live under the peaceful, prosperous, and healthy shadow of the umbrella of universal government.

Before the First World War, Germany and England were in the race of empire-building. For this, both needed natural resources and wealth to maintain their vast armies. One empire wanted to destroy the other. At last Kaiser Wilhelm, the absolute emperor of Germany, started the war, which ended up as World War I, and we all know the consequences. Germany, Austria, and Turkey were on one side, and England, France, and Russia were on the other side. The U.S. and Japan entered later to help England. At last, Germany surrendered, and Kaiser Wilhelm abdicated his throne and took refuge in Holland.

Adolph Hitler started World War II to spread his empire and to grasp the natural resources and wealth of other nations, but he failed and at the last he committed suicide by shooting himself in the head with his own gun.

Nobody can rule this world with weapons, but he who rules his own soul is the best ruler and can win the hearts of all the people during his lifetime and even after his physical death. Mahatma Gandhi and Gautama Buddha were true rulers. As Kaiser Wilhelm and Adolph Hitler failed to rule over the world with all their wealth, war machinery, and slave labour, similarly any ruler who will try to control the world will fail and would likely end up like Kaiser Wilhelm and Hitler. This was not the fault of the German people, but was due to the evil of empire-building.

One superpower is trying to stop the expansion of the other superpower, and vice-versa. The problems in Afghanistan, Nicaragua, the Philippines, El Salvador, and many other nations of the world are due to this empire-building. The wars between North and South Korea and between North and South Vietnam were the result of this evil. The Cuban crisis, when both superpowers drew very near to World War III, was also due to this disease.

All this is consuming millions of tons of natural resources and billions of dollars. The tanks, guns, missiles, fighter planes, and atomic bombs that were made ten years ago have become obsolescent. Due to the development of new technology, the military needs the most sophisticated, modern weapons. Billions of dollars were spent to produce weapons that are now useless, and now the construction of new weapons will require more billions of dollars and millions of tons of natural resources. And so on. Do you see the folly of it?

If this arms race continues, then a time will come when the superpowers will not be able to afford it anymore. I think that time is very near. The hungry snake eats its own eggs. Under these conditions, the superpowers will use their force to subjugate the smaller and weaker nations to extinguish their hunger. Then there would be a competition between both powers to grasp more and more nations. This competition would start a limited war, which could change and become a large-scale, Third World War, and finally a nuclear holocaust. The allies of the U.S.A. would come in on her side, and the Warsaw Pact would join the Russian side. Many other nations would choose one side or another. Soon bombs would be falling.

China and India have bombs, and many countries in the Middle East and the African continent have the technology to develop these weapons. It is estimated that there are fifty thousand bombs in the world. These bombs have the capacity to destroy all the people of the earth a hundred times over. The conflicts in the Middle East, Asia, and South America could become the cause of a nuclear holocaust.

In such a holocaust, everything—men and women, plants and animals—would be boiled like meat in a red-hot oven. This kind of death is the worst death we could ever face. Human bodies would be full of blisters, due to the searing fire of the nuclear bombs. There would be disease, suffocation, hunger, thirst; nothing would be left to eat or drink.

A wise person always thinks about the future and tries his best to avoid catastrophe before it ruins him. Therefore, Universal

People, destroy the evils of empire-building and the arms race before they destroy you! Follow universal goodness and enlightenment, help to form the universal nation and universal government, and convince your leaders to do the same. On the two sides of the scales are the universal nation and the nuclear holocaust. You must choose; there are only these two choices.

Nations like the U.S.A., India, England, and Canada are living examples that people of different cultures, languages, races, politics, and economics can live and work together in harmony. In Canada, one can see Russians, Italians, Germans, aboriginals, East Indians, Frenchmen, Englishmen, Poles, Hungarians, Chinese, communists, democrats, socialists, capitalists, Hindus, Muslims, Sikhs, Jews, Christians, Buddhists, and many more of every class division. All of these people are living and working together, sharing each other's sufferings and joys. This is living proof that people, despite their differences, can be governed by one universal government very easily and peacefully.

Union is strength. It unites the peoples of the world and gives life to everyone. After suffering the disasters of war, people unite for peace, which is a good thing; but is it not wiser to unite *before* the war begins?

After the Second World War, the different nations created organizations for their future protection. NATO (North Atlantic Treaty Organization), the Warsaw Pact, SEATO (South East Asia Treaty Organization), CENTO (Central Treaty Organization of the Middle East), the Arab League, and the Baghdad Pact were all created at that time. But all these organizations were based on defence against this or that enemy, and their tools were military. They were not created for the peace and protection of the people of the world, but for the arms race.

Now, because the nations of Eastern Europe and the Balkans are becoming free and democratic, it is my belief that all the nations of Eastern and Western Europe and the Balkans would unite to create a European Unity. This Unity would create its own currency and form its own military body. I believe this economy would grow to be greater even than that of the U.S., Japan, or

Russia, and would spend billions of dollars to build up a powerful army, navy, and air force.

The nations of the Balkans and Eastern Europe would also join NATO. This would increase the level of conflict between Russia and United Europe and also the U.S. Then Russia and China would have to form a defensive alliance to counter the European Unity, NATO, and the U.S. Great Britain would not join the European Unity and would remain neutral and continue as arbiter of United Europe and side with the U.S. Many nations of South America, Southeast Asia, the Middle East, and Africa would either join the alliance with Russia and China, or NATO, or the European Unity. India, due to the Non-Alignment Movement, would stay neutral. Conflicts and distrust among all these defensive and offensive militaristic alliances would inevitably culminate in a Third World War, which would certainly be the end for all of us. This makes me immensely sad and I pray to the Almighty Father that it will never happen.

As the population, economy, technology, and industry of India, China, Japan, the U.S., England, France, Germany, Italy, Spain, and Russia continue to grow, so does their demand for natural resources such as oil and gas, copper, steel, iron, coal, and wood. If India, China, and Russia adopt a perfect free market economy, then their economy would grow to become equal to that of Japan, Germany, and the U.S. In fact, the economy of India and China could surpass that of the U.S., due to their hundreds of millions of educated and middle-class people, the abundance of a workforce, and cheap labour. This means a tremendous increment in military power, which would result in a serious threat to world peace.

Due to the greed and need of natural resources, all the governments of the above-mentioned nations would approach the nations of South America, Southeast Asia, the Middle East, and continental Africa. There will be a tough, intense competition among these nations, which could culminate in a cold war, terrorism, and guerrilla warfare, another scenario that could lead eventually to a Third World War. And those nations not devastated by nuclear bombs would still feel the impact in the form of radioactive fallout.

We can avoid such a terrifying future only by worshipping our Almighty Holy Father with every breath, step, thought, and action; and by reciting His name constantly and with great reverence. He is the one and only airplane, of infinite size and seating capacity, to Heaven, of which He Himself is the Pilot.

Pundit Nehru, the great prime minister and strong spokesman for neutrality between NATO and the Warsaw Pact defensive forces, created the Non-Alignment Movement with the co-operation of the great Marshal Tito of Yugoslavia. Hundreds of nations joined to stop the expansion of the NATO and Warsaw Pact forces and succeeded in creating a great deal of peace and harmony among nations and in defending the rights of many poor and developing nations. This is not a military organization and does not have soldiers or weapons; it is exclusively a peaceful and non-violent union of nations consisting of many millions more people than are in the NATO and Warsaw Pact alliance. We must learn a lesson from the Non-Alignment Movement and unite to transform all the nations into one universal nation.

At the 1988 Olympic Games in Seoul, Korea, thousands of players got together to take part in the Games. Here was proof of a holy organization. Under the Olympic Games Organization, sportsmanship brought about a miracle of co-operation and friendship. All the nations forgot their enmity and played together in the Games.

This kind of organization is constructive and creative. If people can unite for a sporting event such as this, then surely they can unite for the universal peace, harmony, and equality of a universal nation and government. If 150 nations can unite for fiscal purposes in the International Monetary and World Bank, and seventy-six nations can unite for trade purposes in General Agreement on Trade and Tariff, then surely all can unite under the umbrella of the universal nation to protect themselves from poverty, inflation, and debt.

We must follow the principle of forgive and forget. Forgiveness is the ornament of the brave and wise. One who shows forgiveness shows holiness of the soul. Revenge is an evil that fills the soul with darkness. Revenge leads to dishonour and disgrace.

Forgiveness purifies the soul and opens the door to heaven and salvation. Universal forgiveness leads to a universal nation; universal revenge leads to war and poverty. The era of revenge is over, and the era of forgiveness has begun. The future of our children demands that we forget our past enmities and shake hands all round—communists, democrats, socialists, capitalists, Hindus, Sikhs, Muslims, Jews, Buddhists, Christians, Taoists, Asians, Occidentals...all must follow the universal principle of forgive and forget and must unite under the one and only universal government.

We have five fingers on each hand. One finger alone can do nothing. We love all our ten fingers despite their differentiation. We like every big or small finger. We belong to different political, economic, and religious systems, but, just as our fingers are different but we still love them, similarly we must love and respect all the different political, economic, and religious systems. Love and respect are the cement of the universal family, and we must continue to make this cement stronger and stronger.

When we unite all five fingers, it makes a strong fist; the unity makes the individual fingers stronger and more powerful. Therefore, we must unite all the fingers of the different nations' political, economic, and religious systems into the fist of universal government.

In the body lives the spirit. Fire cannot burn it, water cannot wet it, air cannot dry it. The bullet cannot kill it, the sword cannot cut it, and physical death cannot destroy it. Physical death is simply the transfer of the spirit from one physical house to another. As we change our old clothes for new ones, similarly spirit changes the old body for a new one. Another way to think of it: as water becomes the cloud and when the cloud rains it again becomes water, and by evaporation again becomes the cloud, similarly the spirit by physical death goes from body to spirit, from spirit to body...through the cycle of birth and death. Therefore, the spirit never dies, and it is as old as the beginning of the world and as new as today.

But discrimination, prejudice, lust, anger, nationalism, militarism...all these psychological diseases can crush the spirit of every mortal. Then we have wars of all kinds, terrorism, poverty, sickness, pollution, and physical death.

The cure for this potential spiritual crisis is for all people to join in a universal family and for all nations to form a universal nation and universal government. The spiritual life is indispensable for every human being. Thus, my Dear Universal People, with your full force start to love your Mother Earth and the universal nation, which will guarantee all of you the richness of spiritual life!

No one who has gold, diamonds, physical possessions, or worldly power is truly rich; but richness of spirit is true wealth and goes with us to the grave and beyond, life after life.

There are two kinds of disasters in this world, and people become victims of both. One type of disaster is natural, the other is artificial. Earthquakes, tornadoes, hurricanes, floods, tidal waves, drought, and famine are natural disasters. Wars, terrorism, poverty, sickness, debt, and inflation are artificial—man-made—disasters. We cannot control natural disasters and must cope with them as best we can. But when we suffer from artificial disasters—created due to our mistakes—it is intolerable.

Therefore we must avoid these mistakes, and the best way to do this is through the unity of peoples and nations. Thus, my Dear Universal People, be united and avoid these serious mistakes by creating a universal nation!

It is written in the Hindu holy scriptures that there is an incredible diamond that is found in Amaråvati (Heaven), and the name of this diamond is Påras. The miracle of this is that when iron is touched with it, the iron is converted into gold.

Universal People! Your unity is the Påras diamond, and when all of you touch with it the iron of nationalism, politics, militarism, inequity, revenge, and so on, then all this iron will be converted into the universal gold of the universal family, nation, and government. This universal gold will cost you nothing; no thief can steal it; it is wonderful and fruitful; it will never be used up, and you can use it for as long as you want; in fact, it will just keep increasing.

You can pass it down from generation to generation, and it will give them peace, prosperity, health, and a clean environment.

To seek this Pāras diamond, you do not need to go to Amarāvati; it lies in your souls. When you all unite on the universal level, you will find it in the form of universal unity. Therefore, seek this diamond and use it to create the universal gold of the universal family, nation, and government! Use it to bring universal harmony to the earth! Use it to banish fear, so that we can all think more and work more, and bring constructive inventions into the world that will benefit everyone.

The universal nation is like a necklace; the universal government is the thread of the necklace, and all the nations of the world are the pearls on the necklace. This necklace is infinite in size and of infinite beauty; it shines like a full moon. The universal necklace will throw rays of reflected light of peace, oneness, humanity, wisdom equality, harmony, and enlightenment in every direction and into every home. If the thread of the necklace is weak, then the heavy weight of the pearls will break it and the pearls will scatter everywhere. Thus the thread of the necklace—the universal nation—must always be stronger than the power and weight of all the pearls—the nations of the world.

If in the future the universal necklace breaks, then we must string it again and again; all our succeeding generations must continue to wear it and repair it whenever necessary.

Or, another analogy: The universal nation is like an ocean and all the other nations are like the rivers that always run into the ocean and mix with it, becoming one with the ocean. But still they maintain their names and values in the areas whence they came. All the rivers of all the nations are running towards the ocean of the universal nation and when they mix with and become one with it, they will become known as the universal nation. But still they would maintain their spiritual, cultural, social, and linguistic values in the areas whence they came.

As the water is evaporated from the ocean by the rays of sunlight and it rains all over the earth, benefiting all the people, similarly the water of wealth would be evaporated from the ocean of the universal nation by the light of the sun of universal government. This water of wealth would pour the rain of prosperity on all the people of the world and make everyone rich. As the natural ocean is always full of jewels, other minerals, oil, fish, etc, benefiting the people, similarly the ocean of the universal nation is always full of peace, prosperity, equality, health, literacy, liberty, and unity, which will benefit all.

When there is a full moon, then the ocean becomes happy and the tides are high; similarly, the universal government is a full moon and due to this, tides of happiness will arise in the ocean of the universal nation, benefiting all.

Just as there is one and only one Divine Light, and all the peoples of all the nations always ask for enlightenment from this Divine Light for the solution of their everyday problems, and seek courage, shelter, meditation, and salvation from it, similarly all the peoples of all the nations must always ask and seek enlightenment from the one and only universal government for the solution of their everyday problems. As all people pay respect to the Divine Light, so they must also pay respect to the universal nation and government.

The invisible thread of Divine Light has united all of us by tying together our hearts and souls. Similarly, all the peoples of the world must unite with each other by tying their hearts with the thread of the universal family, nation, and government.

However, we cannot sit and wait for any kind of Divine power to solve all our present problems and prevent future catastrophes. Prayer is indispensable for the happiness of the soul; but prayers are in vain if we do not struggle, sacrifice, commit, and dedicate ourselves. Prayer is not for material and spiritual miracles, but helps us to receive universal truth, wisdom, and enlightenment. Prayer does not support metaphysics and superstition, but it does support our hard work and dedication to universal service and the welfare of all.

Prayer does not need to be connected with this or that religion. In fact, all religions are some of the greatest evils of this world and must be annihilated. We must worship all the gods, goddesses, and saints, read all the holy scriptures, and believe in the universal unity and equality of all of them. Prayer can be done by anyone to destroy the diseases of the mind such as discrimination, nationalism, religionism, and racism. It cures the mind and soul. One who is weak, lazy, and dull, who hopes for some invisible hand to appear and solve his or her problems, needs to wake up, clear the mind, and start to pray. The invisible hand has never solved the problems in the past, and will never solve them in the future. But prayer, accompanied by the will, dedication, and hard work to change the existing order, can lead us to universal truth, enlightenment, unity, and wisdom, which *can* help to solve the existing and future problems.

We can look to the past for examples of this. The medical scientists who discovered penicillin, X-rays, insulin, and so on, have saved hundreds of thousands of people from fatal illnesses, due to their wisdom and hard work. Had they waited for any Divine Power to help them—to make these discoveries for them—they would not have been successful. *They had to do the work themselves, with the support of the Divine Power.*

Therefore, my Respected People! Rich, middle class, poor; women, men; professionals, labourers, workers, farmers, teachers, students, clerks, secretaries, nurses; policemen and policewomen; hungry, sick, homeless, and all others! Work to get the problems solved, and live in the evergreen gardens of the universal family, nation, and government! Here you will eat the fruits of prosperity, health, and literacy; you will shower in the pure streams of universal peace, love, and respect; you will enjoy the calm, slow, and steady air full of the scent of the rose flowers of universal liberty and equality; you will listen to the music of the nightingale of universal kindness and brotherhood; you will enjoy the dance of the peacock of universal forgiveness; and experience the happiness of unity.

Respected Soldiers and Heads of all the armies of all the nations! Assist us in the successful operation of the universal revolution for the creation of the universal nation! We ask that you write to your national governments to say that you are with the people in their efforts to achieve the universal nation. All the governments should give their full co-operation to the people in this endeavour. In the universal nation, soldiers would reap great benefits, especially in their security of life.

The bugle is blowing for the universal revolution! Awake! Awake! Awake! And listen to the challenge. Fill your minds, hearts, bodies, and souls with the universal fire of inspiration, enthusiasm, energy, and bravery! Get up and shoulder the weapons of universal truth, wisdom, and enlightenment! As you fight the universal battle with courage, boldness, struggle, firm determination, and confidence, you will go on advancing towards the triumph of the universal family, nation, and government.

Universal Conquest

The Universal Conquest of Universal Nation
Is a vision of Universal Truth,
Is a hope of Universal Children,
Is a success of Universal Peoples.

The Universal Victory of Universal Government
Is with Universal Struggle and Universal Sacrifice,
Is with Universal Planning and Universal Action.

The Universal Triumph of Universal Nation
Is with Universal Revolution and Universal Dedication,
Is with Universal Unity and Universal Harmony.

Yesterday is over.
The future Universal Conquest of Universal Nation
Is near.
Today is now a memory,
The prospect of Universal Victory is clear.

The Universal Conquest of Universal Nation
Is the true Universal Goal of the Universal Peoples,
To reconstruct their future
As best they can,
And for the best, Universal Conquest is a must.

The Universal Victory of Universal Nation
Is certainly inevitable by awakened Universal Peoples.
The hope of the Universal Children,
The wish of the Universal Peoples
Will certainly come true.
The Universal Conquest of Universal Nation is very near.

Awake the World

Awake! Awake! Awake!
Awake the Universal Peoples,
And struggle for Universal Government.
Awake the East,
And sacrifice for Universal Nation.
Awake the West,
And strive for Universal Family.
Awake the North,
And advance for Universal Unity.
Awake the South,
And proceed for Universal Peace.

Awake the universal students,
And obliterate nations and nationalism.
Awake the universal workers,
And destroy militarism.
Awake the universal teachers,
And exterminate war forever.
Awake the universal farmers,
And unite your universal motherland forever.
Awake the universal children,
And create universal holiness.
Awake the universal women,
And contrive for universal oneness.
Awake the universal men,
And dedicate for Universal Family.
Awake the invincible Universal Peoples,
And run adventurous Universal Revolution,
And receive the inevitable Universal Nation.

Awake the universal women,
And dedicate to universal revolution,
And achieve the advantageous Universal Government.

Universal Nation is the Universal Home
Of equality, equity, and liberty.
Universal Nation is the Universal Ocean
Of prosperity, health, and literacy.
Universal Nation is the Universal Creator
Of peace, oneness, and humanity.
Universal Nation is the Universal Grantor
Of non-violence, forgiveness, and kindness.
The Universal Nation is the Universal Teacher
Of enlightenment, knowledge, and wisdom.

PART THE SECOND

THE UNIVERSAL UTOPIA

Under the Kindness of the Almighty Holy Father, let all the people of this earth always have faith in Him; and under His Mercy, let all of them become invincible; and let these invincible people sacrifice everything in the struggle for the creation of the Universal Nation, and after her creation, continue to struggle for her existence, up to coming ages, up to the end of time; and under His Blessings, let all of them live in the Universal Utopia of the Universal Golden Age of health, happiness, prosperity, peace, non-violence, a clean environment, literacy, and law and order; and under His Will, let all of them live in the Universal Empyrean of unity, equality, liberty, secularism, fraternity, and humanity forever and ever.

SEVEN

THE SOVEREIGN UNIVERSAL NATION

Universal Truth is not to be feared—it is universal evil that should be feared. Universal evil is always eradicated by Universal Truth. All that we dread can be conquered by following Universal Truth. It enlightens all the universal peoples of the earth, and all of them must awaken in this enlightenment to live in the universal nation, the maker of their destiny, the bright future of their children, and the true saviour of their present and future generations.

The creation of the universal nation is actually a very ancient phenomenon. It has happened before many times. And now, at this time, the conditions are again ripe for it.

The Universal Golden Age

All that glitters is not gold. If a small percentage of the people and leaders of the nation are rich and live like kings and queens in extravagant and luxurious mansions and palaces made of marble, glass, gold, etc. and claim that it is the golden age, then they are certainly hypocrites; they would be known as drones, thieves, and fools believing in a fool's paradise.

But it would be a true paradise if, instead, every night every person in the whole world is sleeping under a roof, with a full belly, medicine for health problems, clean air to breathe, clear water to drink, and education for him/herself and the children.

The universal government, with the co-operation of all the other governments, must give top priority to feeding the hungry and making all kinds of health care available, free to those who cannot afford it and affordable to the rest. There are approximately eight billion acres of fertile land on this earth, and only about half of it is under cultivation. In the African continent alone, there are four billion acres of fertile land that is lying fallow because the people who live there have no way to cultivate it.

After the creation of the universal government, the military personnel of every nation must be put to work to redeem this uncultivated land within five years; if this is not done, then the opposition party or parties have the right to overthrow the president and his government by a non-confidence vote. Once this land is under cultivation, then it must be given, free of cost, to all of the people who live in the area. With fifty acres of land to one family, four billion acres of land can serve eighty million families; if you estimate an average family size of five members, then here is employment for four hundred million people! This would bring prosperity, health, and happiness to all those people and would double the food production of the whole world.

Other military personnel can be put to use in building roads, bridges, schools, hospitals, homes for the homeless, and cleaning the slums of the cities. They can help to convert the mud huts in the villages to nice houses for the villagers.

All of the governments must provide free housing and food to the homeless and hungry. They must distribute economic assistance equally to every part of the world, and all kinds of jobs must be given equally to all the people; there must be no favouritism to any group. They must clean up the pollution in the environment and build schools, colleges, and universities, which will help to create peace, prosperity, and a golden age for all.

After spending thirty percent of their income on social security, all governments are still constitutionally required to devote additional funds to the alleviation of hunger and homelessness and the advancement of health care and education.

The Interim Universal Government and a Peaceful Revolution

All the united people of the world must join the Universal Supreme Congress Party,[4] which will solve all problems of the past, present, and future. This congress should be so powerful, useful, beneficial, creative, and active that all people, nations, and organizations such as the UNO, NATO, Warsaw Pact, etc., will come to it for the solutions to their problems.

The universal summit for the universal national government must take place between all the people and nations of the world through the Supreme Congress. At this universal summit, all the leaders and governments must give their full consent and co-operation towards forming the universal nation, government, and family; and the message about the dissolution of all the nations and their governments and all the different organizations related to defence and offence should be sent to all the people through the Supreme Congress.

All the nations, with their governments and leaders, must surrender in front of the united universal people and students and the Universal Supreme Party. If they do not surrender, then the governing body of the Universal Supreme Congress Party must declare a universal election of an interim universal sovereign government. All the united people must give their full consent to the Supreme Congress with every kind of sacrifice of their provinces, nations, governments, political and economic systems, bodily comforts, etc.

All those universal people who will suffer and go to prison for the holy cause of a universal nation, government, and family will be known as invincible universal freedom fighters, and the present and coming generations will always remember them, will sing songs and write poems and stories of their bravery, struggles, and sacrifices.

After the creation of the interim universal government, all the united universal peoples of all the nations must follow the administration of that government. All of them must take part in a universal non-cooperative movement against all the national and

---

[4] Please see Chapter 11.

provincial governments. This interim government must be created along the same formal lines as will the permanent government later on, with the universal vigorous, effective, and true weapons of universal oneness, firm determination, dedication, struggle, renunciation, commitment, selfless service, optimism, wisdom, and non-violence.

"Non-cooperation" does not mean violence, sabotage, rebellion, vandalism, or terrorism. It means not to agree with any of the national and provincial governments and not to observe their rules, regulations, and laws; and not to co-operate with the policies and plans of the present governments until they renounce the evils of nationalism, politics, terrorism, etc. This non-cooperation must continue until the leaders give their true universal promise to give up their nations and governments and are ready for the creation of the universal nation and universal government.

If all the national governments do not surrender with co-operation and peace, then all the united universal people have the full universal right to declare a universal non-cooperation movement against the universal apartheid that has divided all the peoples of the world by the narrow walls of nationalism and national boundaries and by impotent and futile national governments. These governments have failed to provide peace, prosperity, and harmony for their people and are totally unable to look after them; therefore, they must surrender. If they do not, then the people must put their universal non-cooperation movement into action with vigorous force until all the governments surrender.

The national leaders of the existing economic and militaristic superpowers must cease to think that they are the rulers of their people, because these people are now the citizens of the one and only superpower, the universal nation. They must cease to think they are controlling the world. They must give their full co-operation to their people for the creation of the new order. The people will become a powerful storm, and these leaders will be unable to protect themselves from it. Therefore, for their own benefit they must co-operate with their people and not obstruct the way of the universal nation.

The universal revolution is like a forest fire, and all those leaders who try to extinguish it will not succeed; there is not any force that can extinguish it. But the universal fire of the revolution is an incredible and wonderful fire. Those who embrace and love it will physically, financially, socially, and spiritually benefit from it; to them it will give a new life full of energy, health, prosperity, education, and jobs, and will never burn them. But those who try to extinguish it will be burned to ashes, and no one will remember them.

The leaders, being human, will not be able to resist forever; at worst, they will succumb to various natural disasters such as severe health problems from the stress. But remember, the era of violent revolution is past, and the era of universal peaceful, enlightened, and creative revolution has arrived. Any kind of violence will become the biggest obstacle in the creation of the universal nation and government.

I believe that all the united universal people of all the nations in the world will certainly succeed in this peaceful revolution for the creation of a universal nation, and that all the leaders and governments of all the nations will easily surrender. In this way, all the united people will become the universal creators of a new and better world.

After the creation of the universal nation, there would be only one nation, and all the previously existing nations, such as U.S.A., U.S.S.R., China, Japan, England, France, and so on, will cease to exist, and all these names will no longer be valid. All the existing provinces of all the present nations will become the provinces of the universal nation.

For ease of administration, the universal nation would be divided into eleven zones.

1. Sun Zone

The provinces of the following present nations would fall into this zone: Japan, Taiwan, North Korea, South Korea, Philippines, Vietnam, Laos, Cambodia, Malaysia, Singapore, Indonesia, Burma, Timor, and Papua New Guinea and other islands in this area.

2. Liberty Zone

The provinces of China would fall into this zone due to her large size and population. Those of Hong Kong would also be included in this zone.

3. Wisdom Zone

All the provinces of the Soviet Union and Mongolia would be included here.

4. Divine Zone

Australia, India, Sri Lanka, Bangladesh, Bhutan, Sikkim, Nepal, Tibet, the Chinese-controlled part of India, Burma, Thailand, Kashmir on the Indian side, and the islands in the Indian Ocean would all fall into this zone. There would be no more India and Pakistan, so people must not fight over Kashmir; Kashmir would now be part of the Universal Nation.

5. Holy Zone

The provinces of Pakistan, Kashmir on the Pakistan side, Afghanistan, Iran, Iraq, Kuwait, Syria, Turkey, Lebanon, Cyprus, Israel, Palestine, etc, would be in this zone.

6. Truth Zone

Saudi Arabia, Egypt, Jordan, Yemen, People's Republic Democratic Yemen, Sudan, Ethiopia, Somalia, Djibouti, Eritrea, Oman, Bahrain, United Arab Emirates, etc., would be included here.

7. Equality Zone

The provinces of half of the nations of the African continent would be in this zone, such as the nations of the region of North Africa and Northwest Africa, etc.

8. Equity Zone

The provinces of the other half of the nations of the African continent would fall into this zone, such as the nations of the regions of South Africa, Southeast Africa, and Southwest Africa.

9. Unity Zone

The provinces of Eastern and Western Europe and Scandinavia would be included here.

10. Peace Zone

This zone would include the provinces of Iceland, Greenland, Canada, the U.S.A., Mexico, etc.

11. Humanity Zone

The provinces of the nations of the regions Central America, South America, and the Caribbean would be in this zone.

The zones would never be known as separate nations—they all belong to the one sovereign universal nation. Sun, Liberty, Wisdom, Divinity, Holiness, Truth, Equality, Equity, Unity, Peace, and Humanity are the universal merits of mankind and womankind, and it is implicit that they are all universal and equal; consequently, all the zones of the Universal Nation are universal and equal.

These zones are further divided into provinces. All the people of all the provinces and all the zones belong to the universal nation, and their power, authority, wealth, property, families, bodies, hearts, minds, and souls are for the universal nation. All the laws, principles, governments, leaders, police, military, rules, and regulations of the sovereign universal government are for all the people of the earth, and it would work tirelessly for the benefit of all, without discrimination. First, the people belong to the sovereign universal nation, and second, they belong to the zones and provinces; in other words, their relation to the universal nation is primary and to the zones and provinces is secondary. They would have one and only one nationality, and that is universality. They would be citizens exclusively of the universal sovereign nation.

Any man or woman who tries to withdraw from the sovereign universal nation, whether violently or non-violently, must be charged—with or without reason, with or without trial—with the crime of treason and given a severe sentence. The obliteration of these kinds of men and women is indispensable.

The illusive and false names such as American, Canadian, Mexican, Turkish, Chinese, etc., will cease to exist in writing, speech and language, and in all the dictionaries of all languages of the whole world forever. These names are fatal and have divided the universal family into many classes and sections, resulting in discrimination, nationalism, economic crises, and wars. All the people of the earth would live together under the umbrella of the one and only nation, the sovereign universal nation.

National Boundaries

The people of one nation must go to meet the people of another nation on their national boundaries. They must not cross the national boundaries to live or work in another nation. But they should do this to give a message of universal unity and oneness to the people of the other nation. They should carry food with them and sit down to eat with the others. They all belong to the universal nation, and they are all brothers and sisters who are sitting and eating together, as members of one universal family. There they should unfurl the universal national flag and should take pictures. They should sing the universal national anthem; they should embrace; there should be no weapons, no army to create obstacles.

Here, people should sign a resolution of a universal nation, government, and family. They should send this resolution to their respective national governments and to the governments of other nations. The people of one nation should broadcast the message of unity and universal friendship, brotherhood, and peace to the people of other nations. The students of one nation must write to the students of other nations urging the unification of all the nations of the world under one universal nation and government. For this purpose, they should continue to meet with each other on their national boundaries.

Zonal Boundaries

Voluntary movement is banned all over the universal nation. People are not allowed to move from one zone to another without the permission of the universal government, although temporary visits—to visit with family, attend school, or obtain special medical treatment—should be allowed. With the permission of the universal government, persons should also be allowed to open a manufacturing plant, educational institution, health care or research centre, or a voluntary centre to help the poor. The universal government could also give permission for certain groups to move from one zone to another, based on their needs.

There are very prosperous people in impoverished zones, too, but they might not know how to invest their wealth. All kinds of natural resources are available in these zones, but the people have no technology and do not know how to manufacture consumer goods despite all their capital and natural resources. But on the creation of the universal nation, the universal government would generously allow the skilled and educated businessmen from prosperous and advanced zones to open educational institutions, private sector enterprises, etc. as mentioned above. Once these institutions, centres, and businesses are in place, consumer goods will be available, employment will increase, and all this will improve the economy and eventually make these zones advanced and prosperous. As well, the universal government will invest hundreds of billions of dollars in equalization payments to the impoverished zones, which will improve their economy.

But apart from these considerations, people need to stay in their own zones; as the saying goes, "East or West, home is best." The love, compassion, friendship, sympathy, respect, and honour people receive from those at home can never be duplicated anywhere else. People can enjoy their language, culture, food, spiritual beliefs, and rituals only among the people where they were born and brought up.

It is permissible to move or settle down in any part of the same zone. However, a criminal who has been convicted twice by the courts cannot move from one province to another without the permission of both provincial governments; such a criminal cannot move from one zone to another without the permission of both zonal governments and the universal government.

This is to stop the exodus of millions of people from impoverished and undeveloped zones to prosperous and advanced zones. People need to realize that in those prosperous zones there are many people who are poor, homeless, and ill; and their governments are also facing many problems of health care, unemployment, homelessness, racism, crime, illiteracy, natural disasters, etc. Also, if millions of people are allowed to move from the poorer zones to the more prosperous ones, they will undoubtedly be moving towards the big cities, which are already crowded, polluted crime centres, and have many of the above-mentioned problems. The cities would not be able to deal with huge influxes of people, and there would be chaos and lawlessness.

This universal ban will stay in effect until every zone becomes prosperous and advanced.

All the students of all the nations must arrange friendly universal sports under the slogan of "Universal Games." They should send this strong, real, solid, and true message to all the nations. All the students must take an active part in the universal revolution; they must use their fresh, youthful energy for the success of the revolution. But for this they must not use violence; they must instead use the methods and techniques of peace, non-violence, truth, and firm determination. However, they must not stop attending their classes for this, but should participate in this revolution on the weekends and after their daily study times. Their active participation in the universal revolution for the creation of the universal nation and government will ensure the peace, prosperity, and health of their parents and of their children to come; and of all the people of the world.

The students must not rest until all the national governments surrender before them and give their promise for the creation of a universal nation. The vigorous force of the students is like a universal flood, in which all the nations and their governments, and all their leaders, will flow into the universal ocean of the universal nation. The universal willpower and firm determination of the united students will be like a universal hurricane that will destroy all the boundaries of all the nations, governments, and economic and political systems and will convert them all into a huge universal nation with a universal political and economic system.

Capitals of the Universal Nation, the Zones, and the Provinces

The capital of the universal nation will rotate from zone to zone, through all eleven zones. The capital will be in the zone from which the universal president is elected. Suppose the capital is in the Sun Zone for the first term of the universal government. Then, as the position of president moves to another zone for the second term of the universal government, so will the capital move to that zone. When the capital has gone through all eleven zones, it will start again from the new zone, from which the president has been elected by the pooling system. In every zone, the capital will remain for the period of eight years. But if the parliament is dissolved before the eight years are up, then the capital will move to the zone from which the new president is elected.

Within each zone, the placement of the capital of the universal nation would be decided by the universal government. It would make good sense to have the capital in the centre of the zone, so as to be easily accessible by all those in the zone; or the decision could be based on the availability of an appropriate building. However, the decision should be made impartially and in accordance with the circumstances. The zonal and provincial governments are not to interfere with the universal government in this matter, although if asked they can offer an opinion.

The location of the capital of each zone would be decided by the zonal government; again, it would be appropriate to have the capital in or near the centre of the zone so as to be near all the people in that zone. The capital of each province would remain in place, unless the provincial government decides to move it.

No holy place or city of any part of this world can be made the capital of any of the governments.

The universal government must build regional offices in every province of every zone of the universal nation so that people can go there and get their problems solved, and do their paperwork relating to education, health care, jobs and professions, and identification without delays. All the governments must issue photo-identification cards to their people, with the information maintained in a computer database.

If employees of the universal government do not treat people fairly, honestly, and speedily, then these people can enter a complaint against them in the grievance courts.

The Language of the Universal Nation

English would be the language of the universal nation. The language of the zonal Government would be the language spoken by her majority of the people. The language of the provincial Government would be the language spoken by her majority of the people.

EIGHT

THE SOVEREIGN UNIVERSAL GOVERNMENT

The sovereign universal nation would be governed by the sovereign universal government. The members of this government would be elected by all the people of the whole world; thus, this government would be constituted by the united universal people and would be known as the sovereign universal government *of* the united universal people, *for* the united universal people, and *by* the united universal people of the earth.

The eleven zones of the sovereign universal nation will be governed by the zonal governments, which would be elected by the people of each zone, and would be free to make and enact laws according to the cultures and traditions of the members of the zone. But they will work under the administration and guidance of the sovereign universal government.

All the provinces of the zones would be governed by provincial governments, whose members would be elected by the people of each province. These would be referred to as provincial governments and would be free to make and enact laws according to the cultures and traditions of the people of each province. But these provincial governments would be controlled by the zonal governments. As all provinces and zones belong to the universal nation, so the sovereign universal government is the paramount government of all the zonal and provincial governments.

Any time law and order, discipline, peace, unity, non-violence, and harmony are in danger, the sovereign universal government can dissolve any zonal or provincial government and can declare her own rule in that zone or province. When peace, unity, harmony, and law and order are restored, then she will declare an election for new provincial and zonal governments. If the provincial and zonal governments are working well and maintaining law and order, the sovereign universal government will not bother them.

When discipline and law and order are maintained, the universal government is as soft as silk; but in destroying violence, anarchy, the breach of peace, law and order, harmony, and unity, it is like an autocratic and absolute power. The sovereign universal government is an absolute universal virtue in which the basic goodness of all the universal men and women must flourish. Every human being must be devoted and dedicated to goodness. The hearts of all the universal people must be filled with burning universal love for the universal nation and universal government. For the long life of the universal nation, they must sacrifice everything at all times.

The lives of the leaders and executives of the universal government must be simple, moral, unselfish, and dedicated. The relation between the leader and subjects is like that of the shepherd and his sheep; the shepherd can lead the sheep in the direction he or she chooses. Evil and good start from the top. A good leader will have good subjects. A bad leader will have subjects that reflect his or her faults.

One fish defiles all the water in the tank. This kind of leader can defile the atmosphere of the morality of the universal nation. Any person who wants to take part in any of the leadership positions of the different governments must lead a life of simplicity, morality, and renunciation. If he or she cannot do this, then he/she should forget about politics and go into another business. Politics is not for money, power, and authority, but to serve and suffer for the welfare of the subjects, especially the poor, sick, young, old, hungry, homeless, jobless, and members of the middle class. Politics is not for the immoral, selfish, extravagant, or ignorant man or woman; it is not for liars and cheaters; it is not for those who would live richly at the expense of others.

The era of the "military salute" is over. Leaders of universal, zonal, and provincial governments will not be given a military salute in any part of the world for any kind of incident or celebration, according to the universal law of the universal constitution. But they would be welcomed by the children, from whom they can learn the lessons of holiness and happiness. A welcome given by children will always remind them to create the atmosphere of health, prosperity, literacy, a clean environment, harmony, peace, and unity for them. All the people belong to one and only one universal family. To protect the sovereignty of the universal constitution and to destroy the class struggle, the destruction of classes such as king, queen, etc. is indispensable. According to the universal Divine law, we are all descendants of The Universal Father and thus we are all brothers and sisters in the eyes of our Father; we are all equal in every sense and in every field of life.

There are very few kings left in the world. Under the law of the universal nation, there would be no kings or queens, princesses or princes; they would be universalists like everyone else, equal before the universal constitution and the universal government. They would be given pensions enough for their livelihood by the universal government, but the words "king," "queen," etc. must be struck from all the dictionaries of all the languages of the whole world. They would have the same rights as others, including the right to run for provincial, zonal, and universal election.

In the universal nation, first there would be an election for the universal government, and during this election, the nations and the national governments will continue to function. Then there would be elections for all the zonal governments. After the creation of the constitution of the universal government and zonal governments, all the nations and all the national governments will cease to exist forever, by order of the universal law of the universal constitution of the universal nation. Any ex-leader of any dissolved national government who wants to be elected to the universal or zonal governments is fully allowed to do so.

In this sovereign universal nation, there would be three levels of government, the universal, zonal, and provincial, and one person will not be allowed to serve in more than one government at a time. But if a person becomes ill or is unable for some reason to perform his or her duties, then she or he can resign. When tenure from one government is finished, then a person is fully allowed to run for election for any another government. No person should be allowed to serve more than one term in the sovereign universal government in the positions of the president, vice-president, prime minister, cabinet minister, or any other ministerial position. The same goes for the zonal government; and for the provincial government, the allowable time in office should be two terms.

Any person can serve as a member of parliament of the universal nation for up to four terms; but out of these four terms, he or she would be allowed, for only one term, to hold one of the following positions: universal president, vice-president, speaker, prime minister, deputy prime minister, cabinet minister, or any other kind of ministerial position in the universal government.

Any person can serve as a member of the zonal parliament of any of the eleven zones for up to four terms. But out of these four terms, he or she would be allowed, for only one term, to hold one of the following positions: zonal president, vice-president, speaker, prime minister, deputy prime minister, cabinet minister, or any other kind of ministerial position in the zonal government.

Any person can serve as a member of the legislative assembly in the provincial legislature of any province for up to five terms. But out of these five terms, he or she is allowed to serve for only up to two terms in one of the following positions: provincial governor, deputy governor, chief minister, cabinet minister, speaker, or any other ministerial position in the provincial government.

If a person completes his or her assigned terms in any one of the three governments, then he/she can run for election in any one of the other two governments. Anyone after serving all five terms in the provincial government can run for election to the zonal government, and if elected by the people can serve there for up to four terms.

Four terms in the zonal government means to serve four times as a member of the zonal parliament. Out of these four times, one can serve once in any of the positions in the governing body of the zonal government.

Five terms in the provincial government means either to serve all five terms in the position of member of the legislative assembly; or to serve three terms as a member of the legislative assembly and two terms in any of the positions of the governing body of the provincial government; or to serve four terms as a member of the assembly and one term in any of the positions of the governing body of the provincial government.

To serve on any of the positions of the governing body of the universal government, one must be elected by the people to be a member of the universal parliament, and the same condition must apply to the governing bodies of the zonal and provincial governments.

Any person after serving four terms in the zonal government can go on to serve four more terms in the universal government, if he/she is elected by the people for each term. Out of the four terms, he/she can serve for three terms as a universal member of parliament and can serve for no more than one term in one of the positions of the governing body of the universal government. If he/she is not elected to the governing body of the universal government, then he/she can serve as a member of the universal parliament for up to four terms, providing he/she is elected by the people for each of them. After serving four terms in the zonal parliament, anyone is free to serve in the provincial legislature for five terms as a member of the legislative assembly, or to serve for varying terms in other positions.

Any person is free to participate in any one of the three governments by fulfilling the conditions of their constitutions. As I mentioned above, a person is allowed to serve in one and only one government at a time.

The tenure for one term for the universal parliament and government is eight years. The tenure for one term for the zonal parliament and government is seven years. For one term of the provincial legislature and government is five years.

The tenure of eight years for the universal parliament might seem like a long time to some of us, but in a real sense it is not such a long time. The universal nation is very vast, and to manage such a vast nation we need a stable, solid, honest, disciplined, and long-lasting government. The universal nation is a nation of many different geographical areas, cultures, civilizations, languages, political ideologies, economic systems, spiritual beliefs, ceremonies, and traditions. To control all this differentiation, to maintain unity, oneness, peace, equality, and equity among all the people of the universal nation, we need a strong government.

If the period of the universal parliament were to be kept at four or five years only, then economically it is not good, because elections cost a lot of money. Or suppose the universal parliament is dissolved, due to political turmoil; then there would have to be an election before the current term has finished, in which case we would have to spend money on another election. That would disturb the peace and unity of the universal nation—thus the eight-year tenure of one term for the universal parliament.

The eight years does not mean that there would be a monopoly in the universal government by some few elite persons from some special part of the world. In the governing body of the universal government there would be representatives from every part of the world.

The majority of people in any province will speak the same language and have the same traditions, culture, and civilization. Therefore it would be easy to rule over any province and to maintain peace and unity among the people. Now and then the people of the province might become very eager to see a change in the government, perhaps for better performance. This is why the tenure of the provincial government has been kept at five years.

Once a member of parliament has served all four terms in the sovereign universal parliament or in the zonal parliament and retires, the appropriate government should give him or her a good job in his or her field. This is so that the people can continue to reap the benefits of his/her experience, and so that he/she will remain financially strong. The same should apply to a member of the legislative assembly in the provincial legislature. However, if such a person chooses to run for election in another parliament or for the provincial legislature, then there would be no need to offer him or her any kind of job in any government.

When it comes time to give a job to any member of parliament (universal or zonal) who has retired after completing all of his or her terms successfully, then it does not matter whether he/she belongs to the ruling party or to any one of the opposition parties; since he/she has served the people with his/her best efforts without any prejudice, discrimination, or partiality, he or she must be given a good job by the government from which he/she retires. The same should apply to a member of the legislative assembly: the provincial government must give a good job to any person who completes all five terms in the provincial legislature.

If anyone completes all his or her terms in any of the three governments and then decides to serve in another government, and there serves one or more than one term, and then decides to retire from his/her political career, he/she would still be eligible for a job from the previous government.

If a person is given a job after retirement but some time afterwards decides to run for election again for any of the governments, and wins a place, then his or her former job would be terminated. After serving one or more terms, if he/she again retires from politics, then he/she is again entitled to a job from the government in which he/she served all the terms successfully.

But if a person who is eligible for such a job does not want to have anything further to do with the governing process, then he or she is still entitled to receive an adequate pension.

A person who has served in different governments at different times and has served a total of four terms and then retires is eligible to do government service in any of the government departments offered to him/her by any of the governments. In such a case, all three governments are responsible for offering him/her a good job, leaving the choice to the person involved. If, due to ill health or any other reason, he/she cannot accept the job, then all those governments for which he/she has worked are responsible to pay the expenses of his/her pension.

If a person has served fewer than four terms as a member of parliament, universal or zonal, or as a member of a provincial legislature, he or she is still eligible for a job or an adequate pension from the government served.

The Coalition Government

If no political party is in the majority, then two or more parties can constitute a coalition universal, zonal, or provincial government. Anyone is allowed to serve in his or her political party and at the same time in the government. A person can be a member of a political party and/or on the executive of his/her political party and at the same time be a member of parliament, a cabinet minister, president, governor, chief minister, or prime minister.

As there are only two political parties, there can be no coalition government unless conditions are extreme. If any part or zone of the universal nation boycotts an election and no party has a majority win, then both parties should share in creating a coalition government. The party in the majority would contribute the president, prime minister, and speaker, and the party in the minority would contribute the vice-president, deputy prime minister, and deputy speaker. All the cabinet ministers would be divided equally (it is acceptable if one party has one more or less than the other, if the numbers are odd). Both parties should work in co-operation and set aside their party interests to better serve the nation. There would be no need to dissolve the parliament.

The above can take place in the universal, zonal, and provincial governments.

The Universal Constitution

According to the sovereign universal constitution, the universal family, universal nation, and universal government are of the people, by the people, and for the people of this whole world. They are here to serve and assist them in all their needs; to treat them equally; to keep them united at all times; and to maintain fraternity, peace, happiness, liberty, prosperity, health, literacy, and law and order for all.

The universal supreme power of the universal nation lies in the hands of the people of the world. The interests of the universal nation are superior to those of the people.

The universal constitution states that the universal nation is a united, sovereign, supreme, and secular nation. It will not allow anyone to attempt or conspire to split the nation into smaller parts or nations; anyone trying to do this would be committing a very serious indictable offence and would deserve a severe sentence.

The universal government, all the zonal governments, the provincial governments, and the private sector must reserve jobs for all those men and women who are in the minority in every part of the world and must enact laws to protect them from suppression, prejudice, injustice, and hatred, etc. All males and females must be paid equally. Slave and child labour and killing baby girls by abortion or after birth is banned and is a very serious indictable offence.

The three institutions, judiciary, parliamentary, and executive, will work separately and freely in their respective fields.

The universal constitution grants universal, fundamental rights to all citizens in the areas of speech, the written word, association, health care, profession, sports, politics, economics, and spirituality; males and females are to have equal rights in these fields.

The constitution will maintain habeas corpus and due process of law. It will provide for a clean environment. It will allow all citizens to live, work, and receive health care and an education in any part of the world.

The constitution will provide equal justice to all citizens.

All the hungry, sick, and homeless people have the universal, fundamental right to claim free food, medicine, and shelter from all the governments.

No one has the right to claim that he or she is Hindu, Sikh, Muslim, Jew, Christian, Buddhist, Jainist, Aryan, American, African, European, Asian, Indian, Russian, British, French, democrat, communist, capitalist, etc. All divisions must disappear.

The word "religion" and all its forms must be obliterated from the face of this world and from all dictionaries in all languages. But the names of all the gods, goddesses, angels, saints, prophets, and holy scriptures must continue to exist. People must build pantheons (temples of all the gods, goddesses, and holy scriptures) and they must worship in them.

Universal spiritual unity and equality are paramount and indispensable to maintain peace, non-violence, law and order, prosperity, and happiness; this should be the life of the universal nation and without it, the nation would become divided again. Every male should call himself Great Son of the Universal Truth, and every female should call herself Great Daughter of the Universal Truth. These great sons and great daughters must love and respect each other and must help each other financially, physically, and psychologically. They must share each other's joy and suffering and stand together in difficult times. They must greet each other by saying, "All-Satiam,"[5] which means that everything in this world is the Universal Truth and we are all Universal Truth. We worship Universal Truth and proclaim its victory.

---

[5] The "t" is pronounced like the "t" in tobacco.

NINE

SOVEREIGN UNIVERSAL POLITICAL SYSTEM

The chief function of the universal truth is to fight ignorance, injustice, inequality, oppression, religionism, nationalism, racism, militarism, poverty, disease, illiteracy, pollution, unemployment, and so on. The universal truth enlightens all the people of this world and produces unity, equality, and fraternity in their souls and creates the greater good for all.

Unicracy

The universal political system would be known as *Unicracy*.[6] It means the rule of the people of the earth, for the people and by the people.

The political systems such as totalitarianism, monarchy, communism, theocracy, dictatorship, and democracy have failed to solve the problems of the people and have also failed to unite this world, instead dividing it into many classes, nations, national boundaries, walls, and partitions. The Unicracy will transform all these into the universal nation, which will be the territory of all

---

[6] UNI + CRACY, where "uni" refers to all the united universal people and "cracy" refers to universal government; thus, "The universal government of all the united universal people."

the people of the earth and will be non-racial, non-religious, non-partisan, non-violent, and unalienable.

Under the Unicracy, all the present political systems will cease to exist. The members of the universal, zonal, and provincial governments would be elected exclusively by the people by secret ballot. Every person of twenty-one years of age or older becomes a citizen of the universal nation and has the right to vote. No one is allowed to run as an independent candidate in any election or to form a regional political party of any kind.

For the creation of the universal government, all the zonal governments, and all the provincial governments, there should be only two political parties: the Universal Supreme Congress Party and the Universal Supreme Unicratic Party. The world is far and wide, and there are billions of people in it; more than two parties would create chaos and turmoil. The United States is the best example, where only two parties are running the elections successfully for the president, Congress, the Senate, all the governors of all the states, and all the state legislatures.

Similarly, the Universal Supreme Congress Party and the Universal Supreme Unicratic Party will run all the elections for all the parliaments and legislatures and also all the municipal elections for all the cities, towns, and villages. All election expenses should be covered by the respective governments; no political party is allowed to collect monies from individuals, organizations, or companies. This is to prevent political favours that could influence the enactment of laws.

All people are free to pray, meditate, recite their holy scriptures, revere their saints, and worship their gods according to their beliefs. But religion must be kept away from politics. No one is allowed to form any kind of a political party in the name of any god, goddess, religion, or culture. There is the danger that a religious leader might want to spread his or her religion in the name of politics, attempting to crush all other religions, even using violence to convert the people to his/her religious beliefs.

This does not mean the destruction of spiritual freedom or the extermination of the holy scriptures, saints, or gods; or the annihilation of all the different faiths. It does mean the destruction of religionism, which has been the cause of discrimination, hatred, prejudice, violence, and war. Under the shadow of a religious government, the progress and development of a nation stagnates because the majority of the religious leaders are not educated well enough to raise the nation towards development, prosperity, literacy, unity, peace, and equality.

At the present time there is no universal religion; all the separate religions in the different areas of the world have created separatism and many kinds of disasters, such as terrorism, suffering, and death. The aim of the universal nation is to create oneness and harmony among all. If all of us think in truth that we are brothers and sisters in our bodies, words, and actions; in our eyes, hearts, minds, and souls; then we will be members of a universal family in a universal nation, led by a universal government.

The universal government, all the zonal governments, and all the provincial governments would be run by a sovereign universal political system, the unicracy. Although in this system people will elect their representatives, yet it will not be called a democracy. As all the people of the world are universalists, so their political system will be known as the universal unicracy.

Under this system, all the people of the world will have their fundamental rights of universal freedom, universal equality, humanity, education, profession, and freedom of movement; they will have universal rights of freedom of speech and expression, of writing and learning, of culture and language, and of worship; the right to have security and safety of life and property; and equal rights for men and women in every field of life. Any associations made for the purpose of violence, repression, terrorism, rebellion, or oppression will be banned under the universal political system.

Some seats must be reserved in the sovereign universal parliament, in all the zonal parliaments, and in all the provincial legislatures for the minorities, so that they will get their share in the constitution and operation of all the three kinds of governments.

In the sovereign universal government, the president would be known as universal president, and the prime minister would be called universal prime minister. In the same way, all the other officers—vice-president, speaker, ministers, etc.—will have the word "universal" attached. The following would be the eleven high-ranking positions in the governing body of the sovereign universal government.

1. Universal president
2. Universal vice-president
3. Universal prime minister
4. Universal deputy prime minister
5. Universal speaker of the universal parliament
6. Universal deputy speaker of the universal parliament
7. Universal home minister
8. Universal minister of finance
9. Universal minister of health
10. Universal minister of agriculture
11. Universal minister of industry

After every election, at the beginning of the new term, one of the positions must be selected from every zone out of the eleven zones of the universal nation, so that every zone will get its representative in the governing body of the universal government. The universal president must choose one of the above-mentioned positions from every zone. This would be decided by a lottery, with the prime ministers from each of the eleven zones, the speakers, ministers, etc., being entered by their Zone number and chosen at random.

If, say, the chosen universal prime minister from a particular zone cannot complete his eight-year term—due to illness or some other reason—then the universal president will choose another prime minister from that zone. If two or more prime ministers resign or are fired by the president, then the president is still bound to select a prime minister from the same zone, with the strict condition that if all this occurs in the same term, then for the next term the zone of the universal prime minister will again be chosen by lottery, with the number of the previous zone omitted from the pool. This is so that the next zone will be different from the previous one. As time goes on, each zone will be given the opportunity to contribute a universal prime minister. The completion of the eleven terms of the prime minister or of any other position in the governing body of the universal government in the eleven zones at different times is known as one complete cycle. After its completion, a new cycle will begin.

If every term fulfills its eight years, then it will take eighty-eight years for the completion of one cycle. But if the universal parliament is dissolved before the completion of the time of any term, then the time of one cycle can increase or decrease.

There are eleven positions in the governing body of the universal government. In a given term, each zone will have a position. Thus, in all of the eleven different zones, all of the eleven different positions will rotate. In this way, all these eleven different positions will complete eleven different cycles. These eleven cycles can be known as universal zonal cycles.

The universal zonal cycle is further known as the universal zonal planet. The universal nation is known as the universal sun. All these planets of the universal zonal cycles will rotate around the universal sun of the universal nation, and all these planets will receive enlightenment from the universal sun. These planets will spread this enlightenment to the people of their respective zones. As these planets rotate from zone to zone, and rotate around the universal sun, similarly the universal sun is rotating on its axis. All these planets complete their one rotation within eleven terms or eighty-eight years, and similarly the universal sun completes its single rotation in eighty-eight years, so that the universal sun and the universal zonal cycles complete their rotations at the same time.

The day when the rotations of the universal sun and universal zonal cycle are completed must be known as The Universal Day and must be celebrated with joy by all the people of the universal nation. The universal government, all the zonal governments, and all the provincial governments must celebrate this day by giving shelter to the homeless, food to the hungry, medication to the sick, jobs to the unemployed, and clothing to the naked; and open more schools, colleges, and universities to educate the illiterate and the poor. All these things must be given by the governments to the best of their ability, without any cost to the recipients. All governments must free from the jails and prisons all kinds of prisoners, including those sentenced to capital punishment, except for terrorists, guerrillas, hostage-keepers, and traitors to the universal nation.

As we selected the zone of the prime minister, out of eleven zones for a given term with the help of the lottery, similarly we would select the different zones out of the eleven ones for the remainder of the ten positions for their respective terms. These eleven positions will rotate from zone to zone, and in eleven terms all eleven positions will rotate through all eleven zones and will complete one universal zonal rotation, known as the universal zonal cycle. This is done in exactly the same fashion as is described above for the selection of the prime minister.

This system has been created so that every zone and the people of every zone can have an equal share of serving the universal government, without any kind of partiality or prejudice. This system is known as the universal balance system. The leaders of the universal nation and the universal government must always keep this system alive, fair, honest, effective, and respectful. If this system were to be abolished by the leaders of the universal nation, then there would be unrest in the nation and a loss of law and order.

One could look upon this system as a universal common balance, where the eleven different zones are the eleven pans of this balance, the universal government is the supporting rod of the balance, and the people of the eleven zones are the strings that tie the eleven pans to the common balance. The different positions of the governing body of the universal government are the different weights, which are lying on the eleven pans, one weight per pan. The eleven different terms are the eleven different scales of the universal common balance. For the first term, the weighing scale for the universal common balance is the first, for the second term it is the second, and so on.

All the leaders of the universal government and all the people of the universal nation must keep their eyes of enlightenment always alive so that they can read the scales of the universal balance and keep them even at all times. The destruction of the universal common balance would mean the eradication of the universal nation, the universal zones, and the universal government. The whole world would again be divided into separate nations and the people would be dispersed into many kinds of classes—and the world would be just as it is now. Therefore, all must keep the universal truth, wisdom, enlightenment, and oneness alive at all times everywhere on earth and must teach this lesson to their children.

UNIVERSAL BALANCE SYSTEM
An Example

	Z1	Z2	Z3	Z4	Z5	Z6	Z7	Z8	Z9	Z10	Z11
1. President	T1	T2	T3	T4	T5	T6	T7	T8	T9	T10	T11
2. Vice-president	T11	T10	T9	T8	T6	T7	T5	T4	T3	T2	T1
3. Prime Minister	T5	T6	T7	T9	T10	T11	T8	T1	T2	T3	T4
4. Deputy Prime Minister	T2	T5	T6	T7	T8	T9	T10	T11	T4	T1	T3
5. Speaker	T3	T4	T5	T6	T7	T8	T1	T2	T11	T9	T10
6. Deputy Speaker	T4	T7	T8	T5	T9	T1	T2	T3	T10	T11	T6
7. Agriculture Minister	T6	T8	T4	T3	T11	T2	T9	T10	T1	T7	T5
8. Home Minister	T7	T9	T10	T11	T1	T5	T3	T6	T8	T4	T2
9. Finance Minister	T8	T3	T11	T1	T2	T10	T4	T9	T5	T6	T7
10. Health Minister	T9	T1	T2	T10	T4	T3	T11	T7	T6	T5	T8
11. Industrial Minister	T10	T11	T1	T2	T3	T4	T6	T5	T7	T8	T9

Figure 1

In Figure 1 above, T1–T11 represent the eleven terms, and the eleven zones (Z1–Z11) indicated across the top correspond to the zones Sun Zone through Humanity Zone, as outlined earlier.

According to the universal balance system demonstrated in Figure 1, the eleven different governmental positions from president to industrial minister rotate through the eleven different zones in one complete term. Thus, in two different terms, the eleven different positions will rotate twice in eleven different zones.

From the figure, we can see clearly that in T1 (Term no. 1), the president is elected or selected from Zone no. 1 (Z1), the health minister is selected from Zone no. 2, the industrial minister from Zone no. 3, and so on. In this way, each of the eleven positions has been selected from a different zone. You can also see how successfully all the eleven positions are rotating in all the different zones, for all the different terms.

From this table, the universal government can make a real table of the Universal Balance System by picking up all the numbers of the positions in T1 for the different zones and putting them through the lottery. This would cover the table for the first term. Then, for the second term, they would pick up all the numbers of the positions in T2 for the different zones and put them through the lottery. The procedure would be continued through T11.

In the same way, we would work out a similar table for the zonal governments of all the zones, and this would be known as the zonal balance system. In a given zone it will be difficult to predict how many provinces there will be, because different zones will have different numbers of provinces, depending on their geographical situation.

Every province of every zone must get its representation in the governing body of every zonal government, to keep the scales of the zonal balance system even. So, for example, if a zone has fifty provinces, the zonal government must form its zonal balance system table according to fifty different positions for fifty different terms and fifty different provinces.

It would not be very difficult to create fifty positions at the ministerial level in the zonal government. Any zone that has fifty provinces and hundreds of millions of people could easily fill fifty ministerial positions, and with so many ministers, it will be easy to control all the people of the zone. It will also provide an opportunity for the people of every province to have a representative in the governing body of the zonal government to maintain law and order, equality, and harmony among all the people of the zone.

In any zone there can be three kinds of ministerial positions: zonal minister, zonal deputy minister, and zonal minister of the states. These three types would apply to each of the departments;

for example, zonal home minister, zonal deputy home minister, and zonal home minister of the states. Or, another example would be: zonal health minister (or zonal finance minister, etc.), zonal deputy health minister (or zonal deputy finance minister, etc.), and zonal health minister of the states (or zonal finance minister of the States, etc.).

There would be many departments, such as education, agriculture, industry, petroleum, employment, welfare, defence, police, justice, transportation, aviation, railway, post, communications, environment, forest, banking, multiculturism, hydro, urban development, rural development, trade, and inter-relations (there would not be any kind of foreign minister in the zonal and universal government, but an inter-relations minister would see to it that all eleven zones can maintain peaceful relations and harmony).

The position of the zonal president is senior to both the zonal vice-president and the zonal assistant president. The position of the zonal vice-president is senior to that of the zonal assistant president. Positions such as the zonal assistant president, zonal assistant prime minister, and zonal assistant speaker are of equal ministerial level, and all of them deserve the same privileges as any other ministerial level. These assistant-level positions will give the seniors of their departments their full co-operation and information concerned with their duties. The ministers of the states are to assist the zonal ministers; for example, the zonal home minister of states will assist the zonal home minister and the zonal deputy home minister. All of these three positions in any zonal government will work by co-operating with each other as good friends, and all their efforts and deeds must be for the welfare and good of all the people of the zone, irrespective of caste, creed, colour, culture, language, etc.

The zonal balance system demands that the numbers of the ministerial positions, the numbers of the provinces, and the numbers of the terms of the zonal government must always be equal to make the scales of justice equal. If these numbers are not equal, then this system will not work, and the people of all the provinces will not get their equal share in the zonal government, which is against the universal political system.

To keep the zonal balance equal, sometimes we would have to increase or decrease the numbers of the zonal ministerial positions. We cannot change the number of provinces, because they are always stable except when, in special circumstances, a new province might be created, or when two provinces are converted to become one province according to the vital circumstances of any zone.

The numbers of terms, positions, or departments of the zonal government can always be adjusted according to the necessity of the zonal balance system. Suppose in a given zone there are fifty provinces. Suppose there are seventeen departments and every department creates three ministerial-level positions (such as zonal finance minister, zonal deputy finance minister, and zonal finance minister of the states), and in these departments fall the departments of the president, the prime minister, and the speaker. Thus these seventeen departments will create fifty-one positions. However, there are only fifty provinces, so we would decrease the numbers of the positions from fifty-one to fifty by converting any three of the positions of any one of the departments to two (providing they are not the president, vice-president, prime minister, deputy prime minister, speaker or deputy speaker, which departments are unchangeable). If it were the other way, with fifty provinces and forty-eight positions resulting from sixteen departments, then we would create an additional department, keeping the two positions instead of three.

If the zonal president wants to shuffle the ministers of his cabinet or any other kinds of ministers in his government, then he has the right to do so at any time during the term of his government. But the shuffling must occur among members of the zonal parliament from the same province. The same principle must apply in shuffling positions of the universal government by the universal president. It must also be followed in shuffling ministerial positions in any of the provincial governments by the provincial governor.

If in the universal government (such as majority, minority, coalition, etc.) there is a gap in representation for some reason,[7] For example, a situation in which the member or members from a given zone have not been elected to the universal parliament by the people from the ruling party or other political party (in the case of a coalition universal government), for the current term.

the universal president has the full right to select one or more candidates according to the necessity of the universal balance system from the following kinds of intellectuals: ex- or current judges of the universal, zonal, or provincial supreme courts; ex- or current judges of the provincial high courts; the principals, chancellors, or registrars of the universal nation's, zonal, or provincial universities, and so on. Another type of candidate could be an intelligent, simple, honest and moral sort of person, such as a lawyer; or a former or current inspector-general of police or military general; or a leader of various unions: college or university student union, a teacher's, worker's, medical nurse's, doctor's, farmer's, lawyer's, or clerk's union. Any Nobel Prize winner, or any kind of selfless social reformer would qualify as well. The exceptions to this procedure are the universal president, vice-president, prime minister, deputy prime minister, universal speaker, and deputy speaker.

These superior men and women who have been appointed to the ministerial positions of the governing body of the universal government by the universal president, without their election as members of the universal parliament, have the same rights, governing powers, and privileges as any elected member, with one exception. These appointed ministerial level men or women have no right to vote in the parliament on any bill to enact it to law; or to take part in a confidence/non-confidence vote vis à vis the president; or to vote in favour or against any kind of motion in the universal parliament. This is because, since they have not been elected by the people, they have no right to affect directly what has been decided by the people. They can give their opinions,

---

[7] For example, a situation in which the member or members from a given zone have not been elected to the universal parliament by the people from the ruling party or other political party (in the case of a coalition universal government), for the current term.

have the full right to debate on any subject, and have the right to answer questions. Except for the privilege of voting, they have all the other powers, rights, financial recompense, etc. of the elected members.

If any of these appointed ministers is not doing his or her job properly and well, or is unable to perform, then the universal president has the right to fire him/her or ask for his/her resignation and to appoint someone else for that position. However, the new appointment must be made from the same zone.

When any zonal government does not have an elected candidate in any district of one of its provinces, then it must follow the same steps as have been given above for the universal government.

In all circumstances, the universal, zonal, and provincial governments must always maintain the universal balance system, the zonal balance system, and the provincial balance system.

If the universal parliament is dissolved before half of its time of tenure, then that term will be known as an *incomplete term* (dissolution *after* half the time served is still considered to be a complete term). To remedy this situation, the election will take place again for the universal parliament. Those men or women elected to the incomplete term can run again in the re-election. According to the universal political system, everyone has the right to serve in the universal parliament for up to four terms; but when he or she is elected for a term that is cut short, then it does not count as one of the allowed four terms. This same applies to the terms served by the president, vice-president, prime minister, deputy prime minister, the other cabinet positions, and all other ministerial positions.

With reference to the universal balance system table (Fig. 1), say Term number five becomes incomplete. It would be removed from the table and started over again. The new election would take place, and different positions would go to the different zones according to the result of the universal balance system.[8] This en-

---

[8] This ensures that the president or the government will not try to dissolve the parliament to gain more of their own positions, since in the new election, they would not find out from which zones the ministerial positions are to be filled until they see the results of the election.

sures that the president or the government will not try to dissolve the parliament to gain more of their own positions, since in the new election, they would not find out from which zones the ministerial positions are to be filled until they see the results of the election.

Now the table will show Term number five to be filled again as a complete term. In this new elected Term number five, the different ministerial positions will go to different zones according to the lottery.

If a term is dissolved for a second time before fulfilling the time of its tenure, then it will not be considered an incomplete term, but will be considered as a term served for the full time. This is so that the leaders of the universal government will not be tempted to dissolve the parliament again and again for their own purposes.

This universal principle of terms must also be applicable to the zonal parliament, zonal government, provincial legislature, and provincial government, as dictated by the zonal balance system and the provincial balance system. In the three balance systems, the record of incomplete terms should be kept separate so that they will not obstruct the equitable working of the balance systems.

If one or more zones gets one or more of the above-mentioned six positions according to the result of the universal balance system, but they have no *elected* members of parliament who would be entitled to represent these highest-ranking positions, then the zone or zones in question would have no right to claim the positions for the term. In other words, a zone that has no elected member of parliament would not be entitled to any of the six high-ranking positions to be selected or chosen from that zone. However, any of the other positions would be available to represent it in the governing body of the universal government, even though there is no elected member of parliament in its jurisdiction. This can be accomplished by the universal president's or universal government's giving this position to one of the intellectuals in its jurisdiction.

Suppose in Term number seven, Zone number six was awarded the position of the universal president as a result of the lottery. But Zone number six has no elected member of parliament for the governing body of the newly elected government (this means any of the governments, such as majority, minority, coalition, etc.). As the position of universal president is one of the six high-ranking positions of the governing body of the universal government, and Zone number six has no elected member of the universal parliament from the ruling party or parties (in the case of a coalition government), that position cannot be selected or elected from Zone number six. The right of this zone of representing the universal president would be repealed for Term number seven. The zone to represent this position for that term would be decided again by the lottery.

The right of Zone number six to represent the position of president was rescinded in Term number seven, which means the six terms had been completed and the seventh term was about to begin. It means that six zones have already served the position of president six times—each of the six positions have already been served by each of the six zones. After six zones have served the six positions, we have five zones left to serve, and in these five zones is Zone number six, which has lost its turn of serving the president due to the absence of an elected member of parliament in its jurisdiction.

By excluding zone six from the five zones that are left, we now have only four zones that have not served in the position of president in the universal government, and all these zones have elected members of parliament that are eligible for the position of president. The zone to serve as president will now be decided by the lottery.

Suppose this zone that now has the chance to represent the position of president in the universal government is Zone number eight. Suppose before he was selected to serve as president, the candidate was given the position of, say, finance minister (which is not one of the six high-level positions) by the lottery. Therefore, now zone eight has *two* positions, finance minister and president; but according to the universal balance system, a zone cannot have more than one high-ranking position in any one term. Consequently, one of these two positions will have to go to another zone—one that has no such position, which would be Zone number six, having lost its position of president due to the absence of the member of parliament in its jurisdiction. Therefore, the position of finance minister in Zone number eight would go to Zone number six, and the position of president would go from Zone number six to Zone number eight. In this way, the scales of justice remain balanced.

Now the universal president can choose any of the intellectuals, men or women, from Zone number six for the position of the finance minister for his/her government, and in this way, Zone number six is allotted its representation in the governing body of the universal government without any member of parliament, which appears to be fair and justified.

This has happened in Term number seven, and there are still four more terms to go, as there are eleven terms in one universal zonal cycle. Therefore, Zone number six will still get its chance to serve on the position of president during the tenure of the next four terms, and Zone number eight will again get its position of finance minister according to the result of the universal balance system; in this way, both Zones number six and eight will be able to serve both of the positions in different terms.

Suppose in Term number eleven, which is the last term to be served in one universal zonal cycle, Zone number nine was awarded the position of president, but it has no elected member of the parliament who can represent the position of president on behalf of Zone number nine. The universal government cannot choose any intellectual from this zone, because the position of president is one of the six high-ranking positions. Therefore, the universal government will turn to the lottery for a choice from one of the ten remaining zones. Suppose it is Zone number two; in which case, the position of president would go from Zone number nine to Zone number two.

Now suppose Zone number two had been awarded the position of health minister by the lottery for Term number eleven. Now this position will go to Zone number nine, because Zone number nine has given up its position of president to Zone number two. Thus, both of these zones will have one of two different positions in term eleven—the last term—to be served. The universal government can easily choose an intellectual from Zone number nine to serve as universal health minister. On the other hand, the universal government can elect or select any one of the members of the universal parliament from Zone number two to serve as president of the universal nation and government. As term eleven is the last term to be served, it means that Zone number two has already had an opportunity to serve as president, and in the eleventh term it had received another chance to serve as president. Thus, in one universal zone cycle, Zone number two served twice in the position of president, while Zone number nine did not get even one chance at president, but did get the chance to serve on the position of health minister in two different terms.

Therefore, we can see that in one universal zone cycle (from Term number one to Term number eleven), Zone number two had the position of president twice in two different terms and Zone number nine served twice in the position of health minister in two different terms. Although according to the universal balance system, no zone is allowed to serve two times in any ministerial position of the governing body of the universal government in two different terms, in these kinds of special conditions it is acceptable.

But still to keep the scales even, in the next universal zonal cycle (starting another eleven terms), Zone number nine would be allowed to serve twice in the position of president in two different terms, so that the people of that zone will have the opportunity to represent the position of president in this universal zonal cycle. On the other hand, the people of Zone number two did not get the chance to represent the position of health minister from their zone in the previous universal zonal cycle, because this position went to Zone number nine due to the results of the lottery. Therefore, in the new cycle we will give the position of universal health minister to Zone number two to be served twice, in two different terms. Thus the people of both of these zones will get the chance to serve on each position in two different cycles, keeping the scales balanced.

If these kinds of problems of the zones, terms, and positions arise in the zonal and provincial governments, then they must follow the same principles as described above, or as followed by the universal government. The only difference between the universal and zonal governments is that in the universal government there are zones and universal-level ministers and in the zonal government there are provinces and zonal-level ministers. And in the provincial government, there are districts instead of zones and provinces, and the ministers are of the provincial level. Despite these kinds of differences, the principles of the universal, zonal, and provincial balance systems are the same; they appear different because of having different names, tenure of terms, numbers of provinces, zones, and districts, and names of the different governments.

As the formula for the six high-ranking positions of the governing body of the universal government worked according to the universal balance system, similarly this formula will be applied to the six high-ranking positions of the zonal and provincial governments according to their zonal and provincial balance systems.

The six high-ranking positions in the zonal government are:

Zonal president
Zonal vice-president
Zonal prime minister
Zonal deputy prime minister
Zonal speaker
Zonal deputy speaker

The six high-ranking positions of the provincial government are:

Provincial governor
Provincial deputy governor
Provincial chief minister
Provincial deputy chief minister
Provincial speaker
Provincial deputy speaker

It seems that in different kinds of circumstances, there could arise many different problems in adjusting the positions, terms, and zones so that the scales of the universal balance system remain even; but if the leaders of the universal government are discerning, then all these problems could be easily solved. Mathematical skills could be needed to solve them, and the leaders could hire and take the advice and use the abilities of qualified mathematicians. The same could be done in the zonal and provincial governments.

In the universal nation, there are eleven zones and eleven senior positions that constitute the perfect universal balance system. If the universal president wants to increase the number of these positions, then they would be increased in multiples of eleven, i.e. to twenty-two, thirty-three, etc. This is so that the total number of positions can easily be distributed to the eleven zones without any remainders, thus keeping the balance. So, for example, when the number is twenty-two, then each zone will have two positions, and so on. According to the rigorous law of the universal constitution, no one has the right to increase or decrease the number of zones. In this way, the numbers of the zones of the universal government will always remain the same and solid. The universal government can change from one political party to another in any term and at any time; but even with a change in government, the number of zones will never change.

Since there are eleven high-ranking positions in the governing body of the universal government, every zone will get one position in one term. However, if we were to increase the eleven positions to, say, fifteen, it can also work, but not fairly, since after distributing eleven of the positions to eleven zones, four would be left over. To try and accommodate this anomaly would result in a complicated and ultimately unfair situation. So the universal president or government is not allowed to increase or decrease the numbers of positions in this way, but must use multiples of eleven.

The eleven high-ranking positions in the universal government would be selected by lottery or chosen by the universal president from the elected members of the universal parliament from the eleven different zones, so that each zone gets one of the positions and will consequently have its share in governing in the universal government. The exception to choosing from the elected members has been described above. A person must not be allowed to serve more than one term on any of the above-mentioned eleven positions; and once a person has served on one of the positions, then he or she must not be allowed to serve again on any of the high-ranking positions. This is to give the chance to others to serve.

In addition to the eleven high-ranking positions, there are five additional positions in the office of sovereign universal government:

Universal zonal agricultural minister
Universal zonal health minister
Universal zonal finance minister
Universal zonal industrial minister
Universal zonal home minister

These ministerial-rank positions are totally different from the eleven positions mentioned above. The eleven positions rotate in all the zones in every term and complete their eleven rotations in eleven zones in eleven terms. Every one of these eleven universal ministers is responsible for all of the eleven zones, or for all the universal nation, or his/her working field or jurisdiction is the entire universal nation. They are at the universal level and their duty is to serve all the people of the universal nation. Their positions are more senior than the positions of the universal zonal ministers.

The universal zonal ministers will work in their respective zones. Their duty is to serve their specific departments and to try to solve the problems of the people in their jurisdiction. They are responsible to the universal president and are supposed to keep him/her informed as to their progress and difficulties, and to work according to his/her instructions.

They are also responsible to the universal ministers, and every universal zonal minister is supposed to report to his or her respective department and to work according to the instructions and guidance of the universal minister of that department. The universal minister can query the zonal minister of his department regarding progress, development, and problems. The universal minister does not have the power to fire or hire a universal zonal minister, nor does the minister have the right to ask for the resignation of the universal zonal minister. However, he can give his opinion concerning the performance of the zonal minister to the universal prime minister or universal president. The universal president has full right and authority to fire or ask for a resignation from any zonal minister at any time.

The universal ministers of the different departments cannot themselves take care of all the zones, because of their large size; for this reason, there are the separate universal zonal ministers, who will work in just their own zones and assist the universal ministers, universal prime minister, and universal president in their respective fields.

The president will select the five additional zonal ministerial positions listed above from every zone out of the eleven zones. Since each zone will create five additional positions, there will be a total of fifty-five of these additional positions for the eleven zones.

For example, there is just one universal health department, and the jurisdiction of this department extends over eleven zones, each of which has its own minister. As the area of the universal nation is very far and wide, it is very difficult for one minister to understand the problems of any department over all the areas of the whole nation; but it is possible to understand the problems of the area from which he/she has been elected. Of course, the universal president must appoint these ministers from the areas where they have been elected by their people. If there is no elected member of parliament in a given zone, then the president can select one from the intellectuals of that zone, as explained previously.

The five additional positions cover the most important necessities of the people, such as agriculture, health, and industry. But if the universal president and the universal government believe that it is vital to add new universal zonal ministerial positions to these five, due to the need for the universal government to run its business successfully and productively, then they are allowed to do so. But the number of universal *zonal* ministers must not ever be higher than the number of universal ministers, and the departments to be served by the universal zonal ministers must always be equal to the departments served by the universal ministers of the universal government.

The universal government must make a separate table of the record of the universal zonal ministers so that it will know the locations, situations, and actions of all the ministers of all the eleven zones.

Out of the eleven high-ranking positions in the governing body of the universal government, only five of the positions will hold the five different portfolios of the additional five positions; the universal home minister will serve the portfolio of home affairs, the universal finance minister will serve the portfolio of finance, and so on. The remaining six senior positions of the eleven do not have any specific portfolio or department in the universal government, but they will govern and administer all of the above-mentioned five portfolios and their ministers.

When the numbers of positions of the universal government are increased by the multiples of eleven as described above, then there will be an additional number of universal zonal ministers for each multiple. For example, if the number of positions of the governing body of the universal government goes up to twenty-two, then the number of universal ministers with portfolios would be sixteen ($22-6=16$), subtracting out the six that are positions without portfolios, and the maximum number of universal zonal ministers of all the eleven zones would be 176 ($11 \times 16=176$). If the number were to rise to thirty-three positions, then there would be twenty-seven ($33-6=27$) ministers with portfolios; to forty-four, there would be thirty-eight ($44-6=38$); and so on. And of course, to find the maximum number of zonal ministers of all the eleven zones, we simply multiply the number of ministers with portfolios by eleven. To summarize this mathematically,

$M_p = 11n-6$, where M_p is the number of ministerial positions with portfolios, and n is the multiple of 11.

$Z_{max} = 11M_p$, where Z_{max} is the maximum number of zonal ministers of all the eleven zones.

This "Universal Principle of Universal Portfolio" ensures that irrespective of the numbers of universal ministers with portfolios, and irrespective of the numbers of universal zonal ministers, one universal minister with one portfolio will always control and administer the eleven universal zonal ministers (one from each zone) that have the same portfolio.

The universal president, prime minister, and all the other ministers must work together with respect and co-operation as the members of the same universal family.

The universal president can, at any time or place, for any reason, call a meeting of the universal prime minister, vice-president, deputy prime minister, all the universal ministers with or without portfolios, and all the universal zonal ministers of all the portfolios, or any sub-group of these. The universal president can also instruct, advise, and guide the above verbally or by telephone or memo, with regard to the planning, policies, and workings of the universal government. He or she can also summon zonal presidents, provincial governors, parliaments, and legislatures and give them advice on any subject. All of the above are obligated to follow his/her instructions.

The universal prime minister can call a meeting of the deputy prime minister, all the universal ministers with or without portfolios, and all the universal zonal ministers of all the eleven zones; but he is allowed to call this meeting only with the permission of the universal president. When the prime minister calls such a meeting, then it will be presided over by the universal president; if the president is unable to do so, then the task will fall to the vice-president or, if the latter cannot preside, to the prime minister.

If the prime minister goes to visit any one of the eleven zones, he can call a meeting of one or more of the universal zonal ministers of that zone. On his return, the prime minister will report all details of his visit to the president. With the permission of the president, the prime minister can call a meeting of all the universal ministers, with or without portfolios, and must report the details of this meeting to the president.

When visiting any of the eleven zones, the universal minister of any portfolio can contact the universal zonal minister of that portfolio to give advice and hear opinions regarding his or her department. He or she also has the right to call a meeting of all the universal zonal ministers (one from each zone) with portfolios; the minister must report the details of this meeting with the universal president and the universal prime minister. The minister is obligated to give instructions and advice to the above-mentioned ministers according to the planning and policies of the universal president and universal government.

Neither the universal president nor the universal prime minister has the right to keep any portfolio themselves, but if any universal minister or zonal minister resigns or is fired by the president, then the president can keep that portfolio in hand for up to six months until he/she hires a new universal minister or zonal minister. In this type of situation, if the president desires, he or she can also give such a portfolio for up to six months to the vice-president, prime minister, or the deputy prime minister. The president must then appoint a new universal minister or universal zonal minister.

If the universal government has difficulty in adjusting all the ministerial positions in all the portfolios, then the president can keep one portfolio or more in his/her own hands for up to six months, or, if the situation worsens, for up to one year. However, the president and the government should try their best to resolve such a situation within six months. One option is that the president can assign one or more of the portfolios to the universal prime minister, vice-president, or deputy prime minister until the situation or emergency is over. Or, in the case of an emergency, the president can assign portfolios to all the universal ministers and universal zonal ministers who have already been appointed as a result of the universal balance system; all this depends on how the president wants to handle it to preserve universal peace, justice, equity, equality, non-violence, humanity, and co-existence everywhere in the universal nation. The same principles of hiring/firing, and of adjusting the distribution of portfolios applies to the zonal government and its officers.

A state of emergency in any zone would be declared by the universal president and the universal government; in any province, a state of emergency can be declared by the zonal president, who, with the zonal government, would be responsible for proceeding in such a manner as to preserve law and order, nonviolence, peace, unity, and stability in any and all provinces of the zone. But when the emergency has been declared by the universal president, then it is up to the universal president and universal government to control all the different portfolios and affairs of the troubled province.

The relationship of the united universal people, universal nation, and universal government with all the officers of the universal and zonal government is like the relationship between the sun and the different planets rotating around it. All of the united people of the earth have created the universal nation and the universal government with their power of oneness, humanity, sacrifice, struggle, dedication, and commitment.

All the united people of the world and the universal nation together represent the universal sun of the universal truth, which is greater and stronger than the natural sun around which all the planets rotate. The natural sun cannot light up all the planets at one time, but the universal sun of the universal truth can light up and enlighten all its planets at once as well as all those celestial planets we have not yet discovered.

In the first orbit around the sun of universal truth rotates the universal government; in the second orbit rotate the universal president, ministers, and other kinds of high-ranking positions in the governing body of the universal government; the third orbit is occupied by the zonal governments, the fourth by all the zonal presidents, the fifth by the zonal ministers and all the other high-ranking positions of the zonal governments; in the sixth orbit rotate all the provincial governments of all the provinces; in the seventh rotate all the governors of all the provinces; in the eighth rotate all the ministers of the provinces and all the high-ranking personalities of the provincial governments; and in the ninth orbit rotate all the united people of the universal nation.

The rays of universal enlightenment coming from the universal sun of the universal truth first of all fall on the first orbit and enlighten every human being who is in this orbit; then they reach the second orbit, enlightening everyone in this orbit; and thus pass through every orbit until they reach the ninth one, where they enlighten all the people of the earth who are working and struggling there. Due to the enlightenment of the rays of the universal sun of the universal truth, all will learn the lessons of universal oneness, peace, wisdom, non-violence, equality, coexistence, and love for each other.

When the rays of enlightenment of the universal sun of the universal truth fall on the people of the ninth orbit, after passing through the hearts, minds, and souls of all the human beings, they return to their source. Thus they complete a universal cycle of enlightenment; after one cycle, another cycle begins, and cycle after cycle continues to enlighten the people forever. When the rays of enlightenment are refracted through the bodies, hearts, minds, and souls of all the united people of the earth, then they change their direction and do not go back through the orbits of the planets and through the planets towards their source of the universal sun of the universal truth; they return from the outside of the orbits of all the planets and enter into the universal sun. From here they again arise and go towards all the planets and, by enlightening each of them, they enter into the bodies, hearts, minds, and souls of all. After refraction from here, they again return to the universal sun.

The natural sun is visible and dispels the darkness of the night, but it cannot light up the whole world at the same time. The universal sun of the universal truth is invisible and dispels the darkness of the ignorance of our minds, hearts, and souls; it is greater than the natural sun because it enlightens all people at all times. As we are always surrounded by air, and continue to breathe this air, even while asleep, similarly all of us are surrounded by the rays of enlightenment of the universal sun of the universal truth, and its rays enlighten us even while we sleep. As the air continues by the respiratory process constantly to enter into and emerge from our bodies, similarly the rays of enlightenment continue to enter the bodies of all in a universal cycle. As invisible x-rays enter our bodies painlessly and without sensation, similarly the invisible rays of enlightenment of the universal sun enter us without sensation, yet do their work. But unlike the x-rays, they leave us with the feelings of universal truth, oneness, enlightenment, wisdom, peace, kindness, and non-violence. All those in whose souls there is no prejudice, discrimination, hatred, jealousy, lust, and anger can easily feel the virtues of the rays of enlightenment and can really enjoy their lives.

The natural sun is quite far away, although we can easily compute its distance from the earth. The universal sun of the universal truth is also quite far from us, but its distance from the earth is at the same time infinite and zero. It is always in our heart in a minute form, smaller than an atom, and from there it always enlightens all the people in the universe.

Many people do not know of the existence of the universal sun of the universal truth in their hearts, but others are aware of it. It enlightens everyone according to his or her actions and thoughts. To follow the merits and teachings of the universal sun is the greatest achievement of this age; to ignore and neglect these teachings and guidance is the greatest sin of this age. This age is known as the black and stone age, but it can be transformed, by following the teachings, into a golden age of universal truth, equality, health, peace, co-existence, and prosperity.

As the universal sun of the universal truth sits in the hearts of the united people of the universal nation, so have I compared this sun with the united people and also with the universal nation. There is no difference between the united peoples, the universal nation, and the universal sun, even though these three things seem different, due to their different names. But in reality and in their central ideas, they are one and the same thing, which leads us towards universal peace, oneness, non-violence, equality, health, and prosperity.

The president of the zonal government would be referred to as the zonal president, and all the other officers as listed above would be referred to as zonal officers. As we mentioned above, the eleven zones of the universal nation have special names: Sun, Liberty, Wisdom, Divine, Holy, Truth, Equality, Equity, Unity, Peace, and Humanity. Their presidents, prime ministers, vice-presidents, etc., can be called by the names of their respective zones, e.g. Sun President or Wisdom Minister of Agriculture or Unity Speaker, etc.

In each of the eleven zones, the zonal vice-president, zonal prime minister, zonal deputy prime minister, all kinds of zonal ministers with different portfolios, and all other kinds of zonal ministers of the states would be selected by the zonal president according to the merits of the candidates and according to the zonal balance system. The zonal president must select these positions from the elected members of the zonal parliaments so that every province of that zone will have its representation in the zonal government. The exception to this rule is the situation where there is no elected member of parliament from the ruling party or parties (in the case of a coalition government) available; as mentioned before, the zonal president in this case has the right to select any intellectual male or female for the vacant position(s). No one can serve more than one term in any of the above-mentioned positions, including the high-ranking positions. This is to give an opportunity to other people to participate in the governing body of the zonal government.

In all the provinces of each zone, there will be provincial governments. Every province has its name, and each position of the governing body of the provincial government would be called by the name of the corresponding province. For example, there is a province named "Ontario" in the Peace Zone, so the governor of Ontario would be called Ontario governor (or governor of Ontario); similarly, the positions of deputy governor, chief minister, deputy chief minister, all the ministers of the different portfolios, and all kinds of other ministers of the governing body of the provincial government would have the name "Ontario" attached to their title.

The head of the provincial government would be known as the governor. The provincial positions are:

Governor
Deputy Governor
Chief Minister
Deputy Chief Minister

Provincial ministers with portfolios
Provincial Speaker
Provincial Deputy Speaker

The governor of any province would select all of the people to serve in the positions under him or her from the elected members of the legislative assembly, except where there is no elected member; in the latter case, the governor has the right to select any intellectual male or female to fill the empty position(s), according to the universal balance system. Any person elected or selected must not be allowed to serve more than two terms in the governing body of the provincial government, or any other kind of ministerial position in the provincial government.

Serving for just two terms in any of the provincial positions or the first term in one position and the second in another position is to give the opportunity for others to serve in the government. Of course, the governor must select all positions according to the conditions of the provincial balance system, so that every part of the province would have a share in the governing body of the provincial government and the scales of justice will balance.

Election of the Universal President

The universal president of the sovereign universal nation would be elected or selected by the elected members of the sovereign universal parliament of the universal nation either by secret ballot or by unanimous agreement. It is understood that the elected members of the ruling party, which is in the majority, will elect or select the universal president from their political party. If there is no majority, the president can be elected by the elected members of the universal parliament of the coalition of the different political parties. These elected members of the coalition can also select the president by unanimous agreement. If all the parties do not agree for coalition, then the party of majority among all the parties of minorities can elect or select the president. If, however, the president is not selected unanimously, then there would be an election by secret ballots, between several candidates.

However the selection is done, the president must be elected or selected from the zone whose turn it is, as a result of the Universal Balance System. According to this system, after the general universal election of all the members of the universal parliament, it will be known from which zone the universal president is to be elected. After all eleven Zone numbers are submitted to the lottery, the number that comes out first represents the zone from which the president will come. If the election is by secret ballot, all the candidates must come from this same zone.

Election by secret ballot can happen in several ways.

Suppose the president is to be elected from Zone number five. There is one party with a clear-cut majority, but the elected members of the universal parliament of that party are not in unanimous agreement over the choice of president. Then they will cast secret votes for the position of president, and the candidates must all be from Zone five.

In this situation, where there is a clear-cut majority party, the elected members of the parliament of all the other political parties, opposition parties, or no party at all, have no right to take part in the election of the president. In other words, only the elected members of the majority political party have the right to cast a secret vote for the president.

Now suppose from Zone number five three candidates who are elected members of parliament and who belong to the majority political party are candidates to be elected universal president. Of these, the one with the highest number of votes from the elected members of the majority political party, regardless of the zone of those members, will be declared president of the sovereign universal nation. In the case of a coalition government, then only those members of parliament can vote who have been elected by the two or more parties of the government, regardless of the zone of those members. The same principle should be applied when the selection of the president is by unanimous agreement.

The political party in clear-cut majority is that party whose total numbers of elected members of the universal parliament are always greater than the total numbers of elected members of the universal parliament of all other political parties. It is very easy to elect or select the president from a party with a clear-cut majority, and thus this kind of party can create a very solid, disciplined, stable, successful, long-lasting, peaceful, and harmonious universal government. If there is no clear-cut majority party after a general election of the universal parliament, then the party in majority over all the other minority parties would constitute the universal government, and can elect or select the president from the elected members of the universal parliament. But this kind of government is always weak, unconstructive, uncreative, and fragile, and cannot last very long.

In the situation where there is no political party with a clear-cut majority, and there is no other party in the majority among the minority parties that wants to constitute the universal government, two or more parties, or all the parties together, can unite to make a coalition government. This type of government is also unstable, because the leaders can waste time on power struggles, leaving less time for constructively looking after the welfare of the people. This kind of government leads to the dissolution of the universal parliament. The leaders have differing thoughts, ideas, plans, and policies, all of which put the government into a state of chaos and indecisiveness and make its people victims of economic stagnation and political turmoil.

In conclusion, I can say that the election or selection of universal president would always be either by secret ballot or by unanimous agreement, but it will occur in different ways depending on the circumstances.

The members of the universal parliament who have been elected from the zone of the universal president have no right to elect or select a president amongst themselves. They cannot declare one candidate for president by unanimous decision—there must be two or more candidates to contest the chair of president from that zone. All the members of the universal parliament would elect or select the president from these contesting candidates.

If a zonal president is unable to maintain peace, law, and order in his zone, then the universal president can ask for his or her resignation and ask the zonal parliament to elect another zonal president. Until a new zonal president is in place, the zonal vice-president can take over the duties of the president. The universal president has the same right with any governor of any provincial government.

The tenure of one term of the universal president is eight years, and no person is to serve in this position for more than one term. However, in an emergency situation, the tenure of any term of the universal government—the president, cabinet ministers, members of parliament of the ruling party or parties, and so on, can be increased according to necessity.

The universal president must not resign to join another government, such as a zonal or provincial government, or to run for election for any one of them. However, if the president becomes ill or for any other reason is unable to function effectively in his/her office, then he or she would be allowed to resign. In such a case, the vice-president would become the universal president until a new president is elected or selected. There must then be a by-election to fill the position of president, who must be elected from the same zone from which the previous president came, so that the zone can complete its term of presidential representation, according to the universal balance system.

Once the universal president has taken office, he or she has the right to choose or select, from the pool of elected universal parliament members of all eleven zones, the universal prime minister, vice-president, deputy prime minister, speaker, deputy speaker, and all other kinds of universal and zonal ministers for the universal government. As I have mentioned before, if there are no elected members of parliament from which to choose, the president can select a promising intellectual for the office in question.

If a familiar leader loses the election due to a lack of votes, then no member of parliament is allowed to relinquish her/his seat and give the defeated person an opportunity to fight for that seat in the by-election. Once a person is defeated in an election, he or she is defeated for the whole term; he or she can run for election again in the next term. But the defeated person must not be allowed to run in the by-election.

The Oath of the Universal President and Other Officers

In the Universal Parliament Building, there must be a big hall for conducting the oath ceremony and other public functions. The oath ceremony should be conducted by the chief justice of the supreme court of the universal supreme court of the universal nation. At the beginning of the first term, there might not be a chief justice of the supreme court; in such a case, any chief justice of the supreme court of any area can be asked to come and conduct the oath ceremony of the president.

Hanging on the wall of this hall would be the flag of the universal nation, and also present in the room would be the book containing the constitution of the universal nation. The president must salute the universal flag, during which the universal national anthem is sung. Then the universal president must shake hands with the chief justice of the supreme court. The chief justice should hand the universal book of the universal constitution to the president, who will hold the book while the chief justice reads the following oath, the president repeating it after him or her.

I, (name of president), the universal president of the sovereign universal nation, do solemnly take this oath:

I will be always sincere and loyal to the universal constitution, the universal nation, and to all the people of the sovereign universal nation. I will make every effort, to the best of my knowledge and capacity, to advance and support the welfare and well-being of all the people of the nation and the success of the sovereign universal government.

I will never misuse the universal constitutional powers rendered to me by the people of this nation.

With the full powers of my body, heart, mind, and soul I will always maintain the universal truth, the universal enlightenment, and the universal oneness among all the people of the nation.

I will create a climate of universal peace, prosperity, literacy, health, law and order, morality, simplicity, coexistence, and cooperation in every part of the nation. I will give all the people of the nation universal equality, liberty, equity, humanity, and universality.

I will lead an ideal life of simplicity, morality, service, sacrifice, kindness, honesty, unselfishness, and hard work. I will never attempt to be a dictator or absolute ruler of the universal nation and universal people. In peace and in a state of emergency, I will always use my powers according to the rules, regulations, clauses, and principles of the universal constitution of the universal nation.

After taking the oath, the president once again shakes the hand of the chief justice, and again salutes the universal national flag while the national anthem is sung. In this way, the oath-taking ceremony will come to an end.

The universal prime minister, vice-president, speaker, deputy speaker, all the universal cabinet ministers, all the universal zonal ministers, and all other universal ministers in the universal government must take an oath as well. The universal president must conduct this ceremony.

Every minister must salute the universal flag and the president, and take an oath while holding in his/her hands the book of the universal constitution. The universal president reads the oath and the ministers repeat it. The oath should be as follows.

I, (name of minister), do solemnly take this oath:

I will be always sincere and loyal to the universal constitution, universal nation, and to all the people of the sovereign universal nation.

I will try my best to create a climate of universal equality, equity, humanity, liberty, prosperity, literacy, and health to all the people of the nation. I will maintain universal peace, non-violence, unity, discipline, and law and order.

I will lead an ideal life of simplicity, morality, truth, honesty, unselfishness, and hard work. I will serve the universal nation and her people with the full force of my body, mind, and soul.

I will always support the universal people, nation, and government.

After taking this oath, the universal minister should salute the universal president and shake his hand. Then he should salute the national flag. As there could be many ministers, to save time all of them can take the oath together, or in groups. This would be up to the president to decide. After all the ministers have finished taking oath, the national anthem must be sung.

Election of the Zonal President

In every zone, the zonal president would be elected in the same way as is the universal president, but the candidates for universal president must belong to the zone that is selected by the Universal Balance System according to the turn of that zone. Candidates for zonal president can be from any part of the zone in question— each zone will be electing or selecting a president—and the elected members of the zonal parliament will either elect the president by secret ballot or unanimously.

The zonal president will select the following officers from the elected members of the zonal parliament: the zonal vice-president, prime minister, deputy prime minister, parliamentary speaker, parliamentary deputy speaker, zonal ministers of different portfolios, and zonal ministers of states of different portfolios. In this selection, the zonal president has no restrictions and can select this or that minister from various provinces within the zone; however, he must ensure that each province gets representation in the governing body of the zonal government. When there are no elected members to choose from, the zonal president can select an intellectual to fill the gap—just as has been explained previously for the universal president.

The selected officers are allowed to serve in their positions for just one term of seven years. The conditions around the term are the same as for the universal parliament. The zonal president can fire or ask for the resignation of any of his or her officers.

The zonal president and his or her officers will take the same oath as the universal president and universal ministers, substituting "zonal" for "universal" in the wording of the oath. The flag of the universal nation must be present wherever the oath is being taken, and the national anthem of the universal nation must be sung. In the beginning of the first term, the chief justice of the supreme court of any area can conduct the oath-taking ceremony, but later, when the zonal supreme courts in all the zones have been established, they will conduct the ceremony.

Election of the Provincial Governor

In every province of every zone, the elected members of the legislative assembly of each province will elect or select a governor for that province in the same way as the universal president is elected by the elected members of the universal parliament. Any elected member of the legislature can contend for the chair of governor from any area of the province.

The elected or selected governor has full authority to select the following officers: provincial deputy governor, chief minister, deputy chief minister, speaker, deputy speaker, and many other provincial ministers; he must select these positions from the elected members of the provincial legislature, and from every area of the province, so that every area has a voice in the governing body of the provincial government. If no elected member is available in a given area, the governor can select an intellectual to fill the gap.

The provincial governor and his/her officers are allowed to serve on these positions for no more than two terms of five years each. The conditions and principles concerning dissolution of the terms are the same as for the universal parliament. The rights of the selected intellectuals in the governing body of the provincial government are the same as for the universal government.

The governor has full authority to fire or accept the resignation of any member of the governing body of the provincial government, or to shuffle members, or to hire a new one according to the necessity of the governing body. But he or she must always be careful in the selection of ministers so that every area will have its representation in the provincial government.

In the event of the death or resignation of the governor, the deputy governor will act as governor until the new governor is elected by secret ballot or selected unanimously by the members of the legislative assembly.

The provincial governor and all the officers of the provincial government would take an oath in the same way as the universal president and his/her ministers. The only difference is the wording of the oath, substituting "provincial" for "universal." The oath-taking ceremony will be conducted by the chief justice of the supreme court or high court of the province in question. Before and after the ceremony, all the oath-takers must sing the universal national anthem and salute the universal national flag. All other things can be learned from the provincial balance system, which is closely based on the universal balance system.

Powers of the Presidents and Other Officers

The universal president is the moral, legal, and sovereign leader of the sovereign universal nation. He/she is the supreme universal leader of the sovereign universal government. He/she is the supreme leader of the ruling political party in the majority, or of the ruling political party in the minority, or of the ruling political parties in the case of a coalition government.

He or she is the universal chief of the sovereign universal parliament and the commander-in chief of all the military bodies of the sovereign universal nation. As well as choosing his/her chief officers and ministers, he/she will appoint the generals of the navy, army, and air force, on the recommendation of the universal prime minister, if appropriate.

The universal president has full constitutional powers to dissolve the sovereign universal parliament six months prior to the expiry date of its term, if he or she so chooses. If the universal government is disputative, weak, inept, and indecisive; if it is in political chaos and turmoil; if there is a parliamentary crisis; or there is any other sufficient reason, then the president has full authority to bring a motion for dissolution in the parliament. If this motion is passed by a majority of the members of parliament, then it would be considered dissolved. If any grave situation arises in any part of the world, then the universal president has full authority to make decisions for a solution, and his/her solution would be final.

If the ministers of the president's cabinet, including all the senior officers, are unable to perform their duties or are insincere to the government or the president, then the president can ask for the resignation of any or all of them.

The relationship between the president and the prime minister and cabinet ministers is that of elder sibling and younger siblings. The ministers are all sisters and brothers living in the family of the universal sovereign government, and all are working for the welfare, good will, development, creativity, and progress of their family.

In the family of the sovereign universal government, it does not matter who is the president, prime minister, vice-president, speaker, etc.; the honour, authority, and position of one sibling is for the welfare and benefit of all the siblings, and one sister or brother must be happy to see the honour and authority of another sister or brother. The siblings with higher authority must always help the siblings of lesser authority; the younger siblings must always show respect and sincerity towards the older ones, and the older ones should always be nice to them and try to maintain love, respect, and kindness among all of them.

Thus, the president should try his or her best not to fire any of the ministers and to avoid asking for resignations. It takes two hands to clap: the president is one hand and his/her ministers are the other hand. Both hands must always be powerful and active, so that the work of the universal government can take place constantly and seamlessly. In the absence of one of the two hands, the work of the universal government will stall—just as one hand cannot clap alone—and the result will be darkness, blindness, violence, poverty, illness, disputation, and, finally, secession.

If the president finds cause to change any of his/her ministers, it must be done according to the universal balance system. The replacement minister must come from the same zone as the departing minister. The president has no right to shuffle ministers from one zone to another, but he/she can shuffle them within the same zone.

The universal prime minister has the right to suggest that the universal president fire any minister, to change the department of any minister, and to create a new department and a new minister. The president can accept the suggestion or not, depending on whether it is appropriate.

The universal president can dissolve the zonal parliament of any of the eleven zones, but he/she should use restraint unless there is an emergency or that zonal government is weak and is in political and parliamentary turmoil and chaos. If the zonal government is a coalition government and is unable to conduct its affairs, cannot find solid, decisive, bright leadership, and has a chaotic political situation, then the universal president has full rights to dissolve that zonal parliament. The current government will continue to function until the new government is formed. The universal president can also declare any of the eleven zones to be in a state of emergency without dissolving the zonal parliament or government.

The zonal president can dissolve any provincial government or legislature, and in a grave situation he/she can declare a state of emergency in any of the provinces of that zone. But if the problem is not solved by the zonal president and the zonal government, and, due to their own interests, they do not dissolve the provincial legislature and government and do not declare a state of emergency in that province, then the universal president has full authority to declare a universal state of emergency in the troubled province and to take the province under his or her control and place it under the supervision of the universal government.

The universal president has the right to declare a state of universal emergency in one or more provinces, or one or more zones. When there is unrest, political turmoil and chaos, violence, breaches of law and order, insecurity of life and property, cruelty to minorities, etc., in any province or zone, then it is up to the universal president to declare a state of emergency. Whether or not he/she also decides to dissolve the legislature and/or government would depend on the circumstances; at any rate, his/her decision would be final.

When the universal president declares a state of emergency in any province, then he/she has the power to appoint a new universal governor from the elected members of the universal parliament to administer and control that troubled province. If this person has no experience in the matters of the province or zone, then the universal president must arrange a board of advisors of very competent, educated, and experienced men and women from the troubled area to assist the governor.

In any such state of emergency, the province will be under the exclusive control of the universal president and universal government, and the province must be governed by the universal governor appointed by the president to solve its problems and maintain law and order, unity, co-operation, and harmony among the people of the province, and to promote peaceful and constructive friendly relations between the people and the provincial government. If the provincial legislature is dissolved by the universal president, then the appointed governor will rule over the province until a new general election is held and a new provincial government is formed. This appointed governor can be known as the universal provincial governor.

In like fashion, a universal zonal governor would be appointed to administer and control a zone in a state of emergency, until it is over. Again the universal zonal governor would rule over the zone in question until a new election takes place and a new zonal government is formed and law and order have been restored. The date of election in the troubled zone would be decided by the universal president, albeit he/she can be advised by the universal zonal governor in this regard by submitting a full report with suggestions for action.

The universal president can, if circumstances dictate, dissolve any or all of the zonal parliaments and zonal governments; if all of the eleven zonal parliaments and all of the eleven zonal governments of all the eleven zones are dissolved, he/she can declare a state of emergency for the whole universal nation. The president can also dissolve all of the provincial legislatures and all of the provincial governments of all the provinces of all the zones. In this emergency situation, if the universal president does not have enough members of the universal parliament to appoint new universal provincial governors and universal zonal governors, then he or she has full powers to select competent men or women from any area that he/she feels is appropriate for the position of governor.

The zonal president can dissolve the legislature of any province if he/she believes that provincial government is unable to run the province. He/she can also dissolve the provincial legislature and provincial government in an emergency and can declare that province to be in a state of emergency (he/she can also declare a state of emergency without dissolving the legislature and government). He/she can appoint a zonal provincial governor to be in charge during the emergency; when the emergency is over, he/she will declare a date for re-election in the province in question. However, the zonal president does not have the power to dissolve the *zonal* parliament or to declare a state of emergency in his or her zone; only the universal president has the authority to do that.

Similarly, the provincial governor does not have the power to dissolve the provincial legislature or parliament; but he/she can initiate a motion of dissolution in the legislature, and if it is passed by the majority of the elected members, then the legislature would be dissolved. The governor cannot declare a state of emergency in his/her province, but he/she can suggest the possibility to the zonal president if there has been a breach of the peace and a failure to maintain law and order, or if there has been a serious decline in the confidence of the people of the province in their provincial government.

The provincial governor also can give his/her recommendation to the zonal president to dissolve the provincial legislature due to political turmoil, chaos, and other disasters. The zonal president will make his/her decision whether or not to declare a state of emergency based on the severity of the situation.

In the matters of the province, the chief minister has the full right to give his or her opinions to the governor of that province; but it is up to the governor to accept or reject these opinions. The decision of the governor is final in the running of the province. The governor has full powers to hire and fire ministers with or without portfolio; he/she can also shuffle his/her cabinet and ministers, while obeying the conditions of the provincial balance system.

Again, the relationship between the governor, chief minister, and all of the other ministers is like that of siblings—sisters and brothers. The relationship between the governor and the chief minister is of elder sibling to younger sibling.

The zonal prime minister can give his/her opinions to the zonal president in matters of their zonal government, including recommendations for hiring and firing zonal ministers. The decision of the zonal president is final. The relationship between the zonal president, prime minister, and all of the other zonal ministers is like that of siblings—sisters and brothers. The relationship between the president and the prime minister is of elder sibling to younger sibling, who work together for the welfare of all the members of their zone.

In old times, the head of the nation was the king or queen; he/she would be the absolute power of the nation. He/she would have a board of ministers whose head was the prime minister, and this person, along with all the other ministers, would give his or her opinions to the king or queen. But all powers were vested in the throne. Ministers and prime minister could be changed almost on a whim.

But when democracy came, the people revolted against the king/queen, who then became a ceremonial head of the nation, and the power went into the hands of a prime minister elected by the people. In many nations, the king or queen was expelled and a president took the place of the king/queen; the president then became the ceremonial head of the country, and all executive powers were vested in the prime minister.

In the majority of nations today, a president is the head of the nation. This person must be active, intelligent, constructive, moral, open, prudent, decisive, unselfish, determined, and hardworking. He or she must be the embodiment of morality and action, so that he/she can reflect these qualities to the people, who will then also become active and responsible. If the president is passive and irresponsible, then the people will take on these qualities.

However, in the situation where powers are vested in the prime minister, then the president becomes powerless, passive, and inactive, with obvious repercussions on the people. The prime minister is not the head of the nation, and he should not be given too much power; the power should be vested in the president. The prime minister should be available to help the president by advising him or her. The powers of the president are for the well-being and welfare of the people.

In the universal government, if the universal president misuses his or her powers for his or her own purposes or for his/her family members and becomes tyrannical and unreasonable, then he/she will certainly be expelled or overthrown according to the universal constitution.

The Impeachment of the President

The universal president should not be impeached for minor and negligible (moral, legal, constitutional, executive, and lawful) offences, but if his/her offences are serious and on a large scale, such as bribery, embezzlement, drug trafficking, nepotism, violent crime, election fraud, etc., then he/she can and should be impeached. For a mediocre infraction or mistake, he/she should not be impeached, but can be caused to stand down by a vote of no confidence.

If fifty-one percent of the total members of the parliament bring a motion to impeach the president, then the speaker should initiate a hearing on this topic in parliament. The president has no right to suppress this motion, nor can he/she interfere in this matter. The hearing should finish within one week, unless the speaker extends the time limit due to necessity.

After the hearing, there should be an open vote, and if more than sixty percent are in favour of an impeachment, then the speaker must approve the motion. If the motion is passed at this stage, then the process moves to the judges of the universal supreme court of the universal nation for an impeachment trial, which would be held in the parliament house of the universal nation. The members of parliament will present their case for or against impeachment to the judges and give all evidence as it is done in any trial. The president has the legal right to defend him/herself and can hire private lawyers for his/her defence, participate in the hearing, testify on his/her own behalf, and so on. The universal government must pay all expenses related to the president's legal defence, e.g. lawyers, witnesses, experts, etc.

This hearing must be completed in three months or less. If fewer than two-thirds of the judges are in favour of impeachment, then the hearing should be discontinued and the impeachment declared null and void; the president must then be compensated for psychological suffering and financial loss. If two-thirds or more of the judges give a verdict in favour of impeachment, then the impeachment would go to the next level, which again consists of all the members of parliament, including the speaker.

This new process, in which the hearing is restarted, should be finished within four weeks, but the time period can be increased by the speaker according to the needs of the hearing. After the finish of this hearing, if two-thirds or more of the members of parliament, including the speaker, have voted for impeachment, then the president must be considered to be impeached and he/she must immediately resign or be expelled. Once this has occurred, the speaker will act on behalf of the president, or become president, until a new one is elected by a parliamentary majority.

The president must not be sent to prison if his/her punishment does not warrant it. If his/her financial position is strong, then he/she must pay a fine; if he/she has made money due to bribery or other such means, then he/she must return that money to the government of the universal nation. The amount of the fine to be imposed would be set by the judges of the supreme court who were involved in the hearing. If the president refuses to pay the fine, then the judges can send him or her to prison for a period of time determined by themselves.

The zonal president and the provincial governor can both be impeached by the above process. An impeached universal president, zonal president, or provincial governor has the right to appeal to his/her supreme court for a pardon. If pardoned, he/she would not be sent to jail, but would be required to pay a fine, and would not be allowed to run for election again.

Appointment of Judges

The appointment of the universal, zonal, and provincial judges—supreme court and all lower courts—must not be made by any governmental official. This is so that the heads of governments cannot grant political favours to those whom they would make judges. This would destroy the independence of the judiciary.

There must be a universal justice commission, a zonal justice commission, and a provincial justice commission. Members of these commissions must be retired judges of any of the supreme courts. In the beginning, these would be from the supreme courts of the different nations. The judges of these commissions must be paid by their respective governments. In the beginning, these justice commissions would be appointed by the respective governments; but once the universal supreme court and all the zonal and provincial supreme courts have been created, the judges of these courts would appoint the respective justice commissions.

In the universal justice commission there must be two judges from each of the eleven zones, so the total number would be twenty-two; the numbers of these justice commissions can be increased so they can finish their work more quickly. These commissions will appoint the judges of all courts. The judges must not be members of a political party. They will have the right to vote in any election, but their votes must be kept secret. This is to keep the judiciary independent of political pressures or favours. As well, the employees of the courts must not belong to a political party, but may vote secretly. All the judges and their employees must be well paid so that they may not be bribed or corrupted.

The Supreme Court

The total number of chief justices of the universal supreme court should be eleven—one chief justice from every zone of the universal nation—so that every zone has equal representation in the court.

The decision on any case must be based on the majority of the votes of the judges, and the decision is final. There must be no appeal from any other kind of court, such as the provincial or zonal supreme court. All disputes between the people of one zone and the people of another zone, the government of one zone and that of another zone, the provincial government of one zone and that of another zone, etc., must be resolved by the universal supreme court.

There must be branches of the universal supreme court in every capital of every province of every zone, so that people do not have to travel far to appear in the court and waste their time and money. The maximum time to resolve and finalize normal trials, cases, suits, and disputes by any of the supreme courts is three months (ninety working days) and can be increased if necessary. Only the judges have the constitutional right to increase the time if they believe the case to be very complex and cannot be resolved in three months. But any kind of trial must finish within one year; if it does not, then the judge has the right to throw the case out or else make a decision and finish the matter. This way the courts will not become overloaded and people will not have to wait for years to be heard.

The total number of chief justices of the zonal and provincial supreme courts should be seven. If the majority gives a decision, then that decision will be legally acceptable by all parties concerned. The supreme court of any zone or province should resolve the disputes of their respective people. The problems between the people of one province and another province, between one provincial government and another, between the people of one province and the government of another province, and between the provincial government and the zonal government, etc., are to be resolved by the zonal high court or zonal supreme court. Problems between people in the same province, or between people of a province and the government of that province are to be solved by the provincial high court or provincial supreme court. The disputes can be of all kinds: civil, criminal, real estate, etc. A verdict given by a supreme court cannot be appealed in another court. The time allowed to finish trials for city, district, provincial, and zonal courts would be the same as for the universal supreme court.

Minor issues must not be decided by jury, but the decision must come from a presiding judge. If the judge feels the case is too difficult, he or she can hire judges to assist. Major, complicated cases will require a jury, but in this case the jury will not be from the community. It would consist of judges or lawyers. The total number of members of this kind of jury should be five; the verdict would be based on a majority vote.

At the present time, the twelve members of the jury are selected by the court and they are usually totally ignorant of the law and legal matters. Thus, their decision can be based on ignorance and therefore could be wrong.

High Court of Appeal

I have said that the decisions made by the provincial and zonal supreme courts cannot be appealed, because this could badly overload the supreme courts and it would take years to resolve all the disputes of the different governments and people. This would put the judges under tremendous psychological pressure, and the quality of life of all would suffer.

However, in every province there would be a provincial high court, and if anyone loses his or her suit in this court, then he or she can appeal that decision in the provincial high court of appeal. If this high court allows a new trial by reversing the previous conviction of the provincial high court, he or she can go to the provincial high court for a new trial. If he or she loses again, he/she can appeal to the provincial high court of appeal again, and if this effort is in vain, he or she can appeal to the provincial supreme court; if he/she loses here, then there will be no further chance for an appeal. Thus, there are many opportunities for appeal at the provincial level. The same system exists at the zonal level, with a zonal high court of appeal.

The decisions of all the courts would be based on the same fundamental and basic rules, regulations, and laws. Thus, people must not worry about not being heard fairly and justly.

Universal Grievance Courts

The universal justice commission will establish universal grievance courts all over the world, and there will be thousands of branches of these courts everywhere. The universal justice commission should appoint retired judges from the courts. The retirement age of all judges is to be sixty-five years, and after that no judge is to serve in the courts, but they can serve in the universal grievance courts. The level of pay of these grievance courts should be the same as for the other courts, minus their pension and social security payments. The judges of these courts have the same powers as those of the regular courts, according to the legal code of the universal constitution or nation.

No government can reverse the decisions made by these judges, nor can they interfere with the procedures and proceedings of these courts. They are independent of any kind of governmental or executive branch of the constitution or universal nation. But these courts must make their decisions according to the constitution and the principles laid out in this book.

These courts must have different branches to deal with different types of grievances, such as divorce, sexual harassment or assault, land or real estate problems, rent complaints, workers' complaints, theft, robbery, violence, death and kidnapping threats, etc. These branches must be in every town and outlying village, so that people's problems can be dealt with speedily. The judges would be appointed according to their education and experience. If there are not enough retired judges, then the commission can appoint newly educated judges.

In the case where agents of the security services believe that certain criminals are active in their area, but they cannot provide proof of this, and the community leaders will not co-operate, and the people are not ready for a referendum, then the agents can register a grievance at a grievance court. If the judges believe that the agents are correct, then they will give orders to arrest the criminals. The judges will then listen to both sides and if they find that the criminals are guilty of their covert crimes, they should send them to prison for five years or more, without parole, according to the severity of the offence. The criminals are not entitled to have witnesses to testify in their favour. If security services are not taking any action against the criminals, then the community leaders or the people can register a grievance, and the judges will proceed as above.

The judges in these courts and their employees must not have connections with any government official, nor should they have friends among the general population. This is to prevent favouritism. However, they can retain their close friends and their family relationships.

People coming to these courts would not need a lawyer to represent them; they simply must fill in the grievance application, perhaps with the assistance of educated clerks or secretaries, and appear in court. When called by the judge, they would state their complaint. The maximum time allotted for the judge to come to a decision is three weeks; if it cannot be solved in that time, they can refer the grievance to the regular courts.

The judges have the right to punish offenders with a fine or by suspending or firing government employees. The judge can sentence any kind of government employee or private sector employee to one to five years in prison without parole. These judges can listen to the defendant or the plaintiff in private or openly. No media would be allowed in these courts, but the names of those proven to be guilty must be published in the media as an example to other potential lawbreakers.

The decisions made in these courts are final and can never be appealed in any of the regular courts. There would not be a jury in these courts; the judges alone will deal with the cases and make impartial, fair, independent, and speedy decisions, bearing in mind at all times that society must be protected.

Suits against Judges

All kinds of judges, from the universal supreme court to the zonal and provincial supreme courts and high courts, district and city courts, grievance courts, and lower courts, can be sued by their respective governments for wrongdoings and crimes. The trial of these judges would be officiated by five university professors who have doctorates in law and five years of teaching experience; these professors would be the judges, and the majority of their votes would decide the verdict of the court. The guilty judge can be sent to prison for two to fourteen years, or be required to pay a fine, or both. Depending on the crime, they can also receive a verdict of capital punishment.

All those judges who would embezzle funds allocated by governments for social assistance of all kinds would be prosecuted to the full extent as described above.

The Universal Courts

The universal government must build all kinds of universal lower courts, high courts and Supreme courts in every part of this world and Judges of the respective courts would decide what kind of case would be heard by what kind of court.

TEN

THE SOVEREIGN UNIVERSAL PARLIAMENT

The parliament of the sovereign universal nation would be known as the sovereign universal parliament. Usually the parliament of many democratic nations will have two houses, such as the House of Commons or Congress and the House of Lords or the Senate. The sovereign universal parliament will consist of only one house, known as the sovereign universal house of the sovereign universal people—this means everyone in the whole universal nation, regardless of colour, status, sex, education, etc.

An elected member of the sovereign universal parliament could also be referred to by a shortened form, the initials MSUP. Once a person is elected to membership in the sovereign universal parliament, he/she must not change political parties during the tenure of his/her term, because this is a universal parliament involved in world government that requires stability and solidarity of the parliament to maintain discipline, morality, law and order, and non-violence in every part of the world.

A person changes parties because of lust for money and position, and to injure his/her rivals. The sovereign universal parliament has no room for these kinds of unfaithful men and women. As well, such a person would not be allowed to resign from his/her membership to stand for election in the zonal or provincial government. No member can resign from the zonal parliament to join the universal parliament or government or to join the provincial legislature or government. No member of the provincial legislature can resign to join the universal or zonal parliament or government. However, resignation is allowed at any time for health reasons or the inability to perform adequately. After the completion of his/her term, the member can, if desired, change parties, and can stand for election for any of the three governments.

The sovereign universal parliament is the supreme universal architect of the universal law, but she must enact this law according to the constitution of the universal nation. She is the universal mother who protects all her sons and daughters of the universal nation from injustice, inequality, violence, pollution, poverty, hunger, disease, homelessness, unemployment, illiteracy, conflicts of all kinds, nuclear weapons, chemical weapons, economic crisis, inflation, etc. Once the parliament is constituted by general universal election, then she can make laws of debate by the members, so as to maintain peace, law and order, and discipline in the house. Some laws would allow the public and press to listen and observe the workings of the universal parliament and the procedures to enact new laws. She would also enact laws giving parliamentary privileges to the elected members.

The sovereign universal parliament must listen to the grievances of all the universal people and make solid, rigorous, effective, and active universal laws to resolve these grievances. The universal parliament must enact rigorous and fruitful universal laws to help the poor, homeless, sick, unemployed, illiterate, and aged. That nation where the poor sleep hungry, live without education or a home, or cry and suffer without medical care is a nation whose leaders are always dead without death, and after their death are doomed to face the fires and sufferings of hell.

After the general election of the members of the sovereign universal parliament, the sovereign universal government will be run by: (a) the political party that is in the clear majority; or (b) the political parties forming a coalition; or (c) the party in the majority among the minority parties. It is the duty of the government to enact the laws for the day-to-day operation of parliament.

The president will select the vice-president, prime minister, deputy prime minister, parliamentary speaker, deputy speaker, and ministers. The universal prime minister is the leader of the majority party or parties. The universal president is the supreme universal leader of the ruling party or parties. The president is the chief of the parliament, over all the members of parliament, whether or not it is in session. When the president attends a sitting of parliament, the prime minister remains leader of the ruling party, and the leaders of the opposition parties retain their leadership.

Any bill put forth for enactment by parliament must first have been submitted by the prime minister for approval by the president. Under the administration of the president, the prime minister will table all the bills of universal government in parliament to be enacted. All the cabinet ministers with and without different portfolios will co-operatively assist the prime minister in this matter and all other kinds of matters related to the parliament and to the universal government. The prime minister and all the other ministers have the right to ask, and reply to, questions of the members of parliament of all the opposition parties. When the president is attending a sitting of parliament, he also is required to reply to questions submitted by the members. The speaker should be neutral, being the presiding officer of the parliament.

A member who has been elected for the universal parliament and who has committed a crime must not be arrested while in the house; but he or she can be arrested when he or she exits. The guilty member is not allowed to continue sitting in parliament to avoid arrest, and must leave the house when the others leave.

None of the senior government officers, from president to members of parliament, should be charged for minor errors; it is human to err, and no one is perfect. No member of parliament should be charged for any kind of debate or questions asked or answered in the house. He or she is allowed verbal attacks or criticisms of policies or ideas. However, no abuse of members is allowed, no horseplay, no violence of any kind. Members can be charged for cheating, treason, corruption, blackmail, black market activity, drug trafficking, embezzlement, racketeering, and so on.

Each sitting of parliament must begin with the singing of the universal national anthem. Parliament should keep a record of the Hansards. The government would form committees to handle justice, finance, medicine, industry, education, agriculture, housing, employment, etc. There should be four representatives from the office of the president to report to the president on parliamentary affairs.

Every bill that has to be enacted as a law should pass through three readings, as it is now done in every parliament. If the majority of a secret vote goes in its favour, then the prime minister should send it to the president for final signature, after which it becomes law. The president and the speaker should also vote on this bill. It is up to the ruling party or parties as to whether to conduct a secret or open vote.

The House of the Sovereign Universal Parliament

This is a universal house of universal truth, morality, simplicity, enlightenment, liberty, justice, fraternity, unity, peace, renunciation, and equality. No member or employee of the parliament, employee of the press, or any other civilian can be allowed to enter this house if he/she is intoxicated or under any kind of narcotic influence. Provocative clothing must not be allowed in the house. The morality and discipline of the house must be maintained at all times, and the universal speaker has full authority to expel those who do not comply with the rules. The universal government can heavily fine those who threaten the morality or discipline of the house. The universal government will establish the sitting times and period of the parliament and has the right to summon the parliament for a special session in the house at any time.

The buildings of the universal, zonal, and provincial governments must not be full of luxuries, pomp, or show, but must be simple, strong, safe, and secure.

The house should be built with two large chambers, one for the ruling party or parties, and the other for the opposition parties. The chamber for the opposition parties can be divided into many rooms to accommodate all of the parties. In the centre of the house and to one side there should be a big chair for the universal speaker. On the other side there should be three more chairs, also large, but the central one should be larger than the other two—this one would be for the universal president. The chair to the right of the president would be for the vice-president and the one on the left for the universal prime minister. This arrangement is to allow the vice-president and the prime minister to assist the president with the affairs of government. The universal flag must hang to the right of the three chairs, and the universal national anthem must be displayed to their left.

There should be a table in the centre of the house, and on this table should rest a copy of the sovereign universal constitution, a candle, and a common balance. The candle is a symbol of enlightenment and must be lit at all times. The common balance is a symbol of equity and justice. The presence of a copy of the constitution reminds the members of parliament to follow the principles contained therein.

The House of the Zonal Parliament

The house of the zonal parliament would be known as the zonal parliament house. The type of construction of this house would be the same as that of the house of the sovereign universal parliament. When the time comes to place many nations in one zone, many houses of parliament will be left vacant, and the zonal government can use these buildings, renovating them to fit the new requirements. All of the rules and regulations of the zonal parliament house would be the same as those of the house of the universal parliament. The flag, the national anthem, the table with the candle, balance, and constitution—all would be as they are in the house of the universal parliament.

Beside all parliament houses and offices of all the government officials, there must be built temples, called pantheons (but not churches, gurudwaras, mosques, synagogues, etc.), of all the gods and goddesses where holy scriptures must be read in the English language so that all may understand them. All members of parliament and other government officials must attend these temples for an hour each working day and listen carefully and quietly to these scriptures before they start their official duties. Any member who fails to attend can be fined by the speaker or head of the government from one hundred to three hundred dollars. Exceptions would be made for illness, a family member's illness, spiritual ceremonies such as weddings, funerals, etc., or official duties. This is to keep them on a spiritual plane so that they can be fair, honest, and truthful in their duties.

For hundreds of years, almost all the leaders of the nations have not been divine or spiritual, and therefore the world has been plagued by all sorts of natural disasters and human crimes. By attending the pantheons every day, all these leaders, ministers, and their executives would become divine, and then the people would follow. In this positive and divine world, natural disasters and crime would disappear forever.

The House of the Provincial Legislature
The house of the provincial legislature should be known as the provincial legislature house. As all the provinces of all the nations will become the provinces of the universal nation, of the eleven zones, the buildings that were being used by the provincial legislature can continue to be used by them, under the administration of the zonal and universal governments. Again, some renovations can be done to make the appearance of the existing buildings compatible with the other governmental houses. Again, all of the rules and regulations of the provincial legislature house would be the same as those of the house of the universal parliament; and the flag, the national anthem, the table with the candle, balance, and constitution—all would be as they are in the house of the universal parliament.

The Universal, Zonal, and Provincial Electoral Commission
The governments would appoint electoral commissions to conduct elections for the members of the universal and zonal parliaments and provincial legislatures. These commissions would execute their duties according to the same methods as are cur-

rently being employed in any democratic nation and would decide who is eligible to be a candidate for election.

The Numbers of Members of Parliament and Legislature

The total number of universal parliament members should be 781 (11 x 71), of the zonal parliament members, 575, and of the provincial legislature members, 275. These are always odd numbers so that one party is always in the majority. The numbers can be decreased by the decision of the respective governments; but to increase the numbers, there must be a vote taken by the parliament or legislature, with a 60% majority in favour.

The Dissolution of the Sovereign Universal Parliament

The universal president has the prerogative, if he/she deems it to be appropriate, to dissolve the sovereign universal parliament six months or less prior to its expiry date. He or she can put forth the motion for dissolution in parliament, and if this motion is passed by the majority of the elected members, parliament will be dissolved.

If the universal government is weak and unable to perform its functions successfully, or the nation is in political turmoil, or there is a parliamentary crisis, and the government is unable to make the right decisions, then this would be an appropriate time for the president to call for dissolution of parliament.

If the leader of the opposition party (it is understood that there could be more than one opposition party and leader) believes that the dissolution of the universal parliament is vital, and there are political or parliamentary crises, and the universal government of the ruling party is not conducting its national affairs in an appropriate manner, and there is no decisive leader in that government, then he/she can put forth a motion in the house for dissolution of the universal parliament. This type of motion must be signed by thirty percent of the total elected members of the universal parliament. Once signed, the universal speaker must put forth this motion in the house, and the universal president and his/her government have no right to refuse it. If this motion is passed by a majority of the elected members, then the president must declare the dissolution of the universal parliament.

If the universal president and government become autocratic, despotic, and tyrannical, and are performing unconstitutional, illegal, unjust, or inhumane actions, and they fail to maintain peace, law and order, unity, and discipline in the universal nation, then the leader of the opposition party can bring the motion of dissolution of the parliament. This motion must be signed by thirty percent of the elected members, and in this scenario, the speaker must conduct this motion without delay. This cannot be blocked by the president or his/her government. If this motion is passed by a majority of the elected members, then the president must declare the dissolution of the universal parliament.

After the dissolution of the universal parliament, the universal president and his/her ministers must remain in power until a new universal government is formed. If any one of them becomes unable to function due to illness or other reasons, the president can appoint another minister to fill the gap. The nation must never be left without a functioning government.

Within six months after the dissolution of the universal parliament, the president must declare a date for the new universal general election for the formation of the new universal parliament and government.

The universal president and all his/her ministers are responsible to the universal parliament for their actions and the fulfillment of their duties. The leader of the opposition party (or leaders of the opposition parties) can request the resignation of the universal president or any of his/her ministers if they are failing to perform their duties in the government. However, in this situation it is the decision of the president whether to resign, and it is up to the president to ask these ministers to resign. Of course, any minister who seriously blunders must resign, and if he/she fails to do so, the president must insist on his/her resignation.

The Zonal Parliament

The parliament of any zone would be known as the zonal parliament, and the head of the zonal government would be known as the zonal president. The business of the zonal parliament would be conducted in the same manner as the universal parliament.

The zonal parliament would be dissolved in the same way as the universal parliament. In the event of an emergency situation, zonal parliamentary crisis, zonal governmental crisis, or the breach of law and order, discipline, unity, and peace, the universal president has the power to dissolve the zonal parliament and zonal government.

The Provincial Legislature

The provincial legislature would function in the same manner as the universal and zonal parliaments. The head of the provincial government is known as the provincial governor. In the event of an emergency situation, provincial legislature crisis, provincial governmental crisis, or the breach of law and order, the zonal president has the power to dissolve the provincial legislature. If for some reason the zonal president does not do so, the universal president has the prerogative to dissolve the provincial legislature and government.

Qualifications of Candidates for a Seat in Parliament

Only an educated person can lead his or her constituents towards universality, equality, liberty, fraternity, justice, peace, prosperity, health, a clean environment, and law and order. The following should be the qualifications of a candidate:

1. Any male or female with a doctorate in economics or political science, or a Ph.D. degree or its equivalent, in medicine, engineering, social sciences, mathematics, literature, science, etc., and an excellent record can be a candidate. If no such person is available, then someone can run who has an A or B+ average in political science, economics, or law from a university.

   At the beginning, for the first two terms of all the governments, anyone who wants to be a candidate for election to any parliament or legislature can run if he or she has a Ph.D. in any of the university subjects— with the exception of any kind of religion—and five years' teaching experience.

2. He or she must have at least five years of teaching experience in one of the above-mentioned subjects in a university or in a college affiliated with, or recognized by, a university and have an excellent mastery of the English language.

3. He or she must not be a drug addict, an alcoholic, a gambler, or involved in any way with pornography. He/she must not believe in divorce, abortion, hatred, discrimination, prejudice, or racism of any kind.

4. He/she must not have the desire to rule over the world or any part of the world, but must instead have a desire to serve all the people of the world, especially the poor, homeless, sick, hungry, and battered women and children, and must show it by positive action.

5. He/she must believe in the philosophy as written in this book, *Inevitable and Invincible*, must have a thorough knowledge of its contents, and must show respect for it.

6. He or she must not have any serious kind of criminal record and he/she must be categorically honest.

7. He/she must not try to win any kind of election by unfair means.

8. He/she, or his or her immediate family, must not own a private sector corporation or any kind of large-scale business. A lawyer who runs his or her own law practice or works for private or public sector enterprises is not allowed to run for election.

9. He or she must not covertly or openly operate businesses in pornography, prostitution, trafficking, or the manufacture and sale of alcoholic beverages; and must not earn money by granting favours to the wealthy or to business people.

10. He or she must not be involved in the movie industry in any capacity, or be a writer of music or literary works for that industry; or be involved in any way with beauty contests. He/she must not live the lifestyle of the rich and famous.

Duties of the Universal Vice-President

The vice-president will conduct the special sessions of the universal parliament in the absence of the president. He or she will visit different areas of the world and will inform the president of problems and grievances. He/she will inaugurate the main projects in the absence of the president, in the name of the president. He/she must be active and intelligent and must be aware of what is going on in the world. He/she must ensure that all parts of the world are being dealt with fairly, honestly, and equally, especially in the distribution of the money, welfare benefits, and creative projects for the eradication of poverty. He/she is responsible for awarding prizes to eminent scientists, engineers, doctors, writers, teachers, etc. in the absence of the president. If the president dies or resigns, the vice-president will automatically take on the role of president until a new one is elected by the constitutional procedure.

The same kinds of duties would be taken on by the zonal vice-president of each zone, and by the provincial deputy governor in the provinces.

The Duties of the Universal, Zonal, and Provincial Speakers

The duties of the universal speaker would be the same as those of any speaker in any democratic parliament. He or she would, on behalf of the universal parliament, appoint the elected leader of the majority political party or parties as the universal president. At the request of the leader(s) of the opposition party or parties, he/she would call a special sitting of the parliament to conduct the motion of dissolution of the universal parliament, or a non-confidence vote against the universal government, or a non-confidence vote against the universal president.

The duties of the zonal speaker on the zonal level and of the provincial speaker on the provincial level would be the same as those of the universal speaker on the universal level.

The Duties of the Universal Prime Minister

The universal prime minister is the leader of the ruling party, or parties in a coalition government, and the leader of the universal government. It is his or her role to provide the universal president with his/her opinions vis-à-vis government policies and planning. He/she would suggest new bills; inform the president about problems and situations in different parts of the world and about conditions in the provinces and zones; recommend hiring or firing of ministers in his/her department; answer all the questions in the house put forth by the opposition parties; keep the president informed about parliamentary matters. The prime minister is the shadow of the president.

The prime minister will give recommendations to the president vis-à-vis dissolving zonal or provincial governments, zonal parliaments, or provincial legislatures. He or she can suggest to the president a motion of dissolution of the sovereign universal parliament. He or she can, if it is appropriate, recommend declaring a state of emergency in any area of the nation, or in the whole nation.

The Duties of the Zonal Prime Minister

The zonal prime minister can recommend to the zonal president the hiring or firing of any zonal minister of any department. He or she is the leader of the ruling party or parties of the zonal parliament. He/she makes policies and plans and creates bills and gets them approved by the zonal president. The bills will be presented to the zonal parliament for enactment.

The zonal president is the supreme leader of the ruling party or parties. When the zonal president attends a session of the zonal parliament, then he/she is the chief of the zonal parliament, including all the members. The zonal prime minister can recommend that the president dissolve the provincial government and/or legislature; or to declare a state of emergency in certain provinces in the zone, or in the whole zone.

The Duties of the Provincial Chief Minister

This person would give his or her opinions to the provincial government vis-à-vis hiring or firing any of the provincial ministers. He or she is the leader of the ruling party or parties. The provincial governor is the supreme leader of the ruling party or parties; he or she is also the chief of the provincial legislature whenever it is in session. The chief minister keeps the governor apprised of the situation of law and order in the province. He or she will work on bills to get them enacted by the legislature, after having gotten the approval of the governor.

The State of Emergency

When in any part of the world there is a breakdown of discipline, unity, peace, law and order, etc., and the situation becomes grave, the universal president can declare a state of emergency in that part of the universal nation. This could be a trouble-ridden province or even a whole zone. The universal president will declare universal presidential rule in the area in question. For a province, he/she will appoint a universal provincial governor who will act exclusively according to the guidance and directions issued by the universal government; for a zone, the universal president will appoint a universal zonal governor who will work in that zone under the exclusive guidance of the universal government and will submit progress reports to the universal government.

The declaration of a state of emergency in any zone does not automatically cause the universal president to dissolve the zonal parliament, and any kind of condition can be resolved without the prorogation of the zonal parliament. The universal president and government will decide the length of time the state of emergency of any zone or province will remain in effect, depending on the conditions in the troubled area.

The universal president will have the right to increase the numbers of ministers without recourse to the universal balance system and can shuffle his or her ministers between zones or departments. He or she can create new departments as needed. However, once the emergency is over, the government must revert to the universal balance system and must restore law and order in the nation according to the universal constitution.

When a state of emergency is declared in any zone or province, then all those rights of the people that are routinely rescinded by the government of any democratic nation in a state of emergency would be rescinded temporarily by the universal president or government, or by the zonal president or government if appropriate.

If the entire universal nation enters into a condition whereby peace, law and order, unity, co-operation, and discipline have been threatened, then the universal president has full authority to declare a universal state of emergency. The universal president can suspend freedom of the press, and can suspend the rights and freedoms of all the people in the nation. The press and the public would no longer be allowed to attend sittings of parliament; and some or all newspapers might be suspended. Broadcasting media such as radio and television would be restricted to reporting only such news and information as would be provided by the universal president and government.

In the interests of restoring peace, discipline, and harmony, the universal president can call special sessions of parliament; cut short the period of debate; stop elections in the provinces; enact laws without the approval of parliament; ban all unions, seal their bank accounts,[9] confiscate their property, and detain their leaders and members; suspend the right of association, such that two or more individuals are not to gather in a group; declare a curfew in any part of the world; ban religious activities and detain religious leaders, indicting them if they are guilty of a crime or misdemeanour; and suspend all travel of individuals.

The universal president and government will have the right to move police personnel to whatever part of the world is in need of assistance. As well, they can declare martial law in those areas of the universal nation where the situation is out of control and cannot be handled by the civilian authorities and police. If the whole nation is in chaos, they can declare martial law for the entire world. In any area—or the whole nation—where peace and consistent law and order have returned, the martial law can be lifted, even before the state of emergency has been lifted.

In this situation, he/she can dissolve all of the zonal and provincial governments and legislatures and have them all revert to his/her administration, and would have the right to appoint

---

[9] If the banks do not co-operate in these matters, then the people who are in charge can be detained by the universal president and government. If they are guilty, they can be indicted.

universal zonal and provincial governors; but might prefer that they continue to function. The president can dissolve some and not others, if this is indicated.

The universal president can arrest those men and women who are the cause of the breach of law and order and can give them appropriate sentences with or without trial, according to the constitution of the universal nation. If it happens that the elected members of the parliament of the universal nation of the opposition parties and their respective leaders are instigating a breach of law and order, peace, harmony, etc., then the universal president can arrest some or all of them and has the right to detain them until the state of emergency has been lifted. If, after the emergency is over, the universal president or government believes there is enough proof to indict some or all of them, then the government has the right to file a suit against them; or to curtail their sentence.

Clear-cut majority zonal government

Suppose in a given zone a general election has taken place, and the new zonal parliament has begun its seven-year term. One political party has a clear-cut majority and that party constitutes the zonal government. But after one year, some problems have begun to arise, and the zonal government tries to resolve them without success. Law and order, peace, unity, and discipline are endangered. The universal government allows a year for the zonal government to solve its problems, again without success. To control this situation, the universal president might consider declaring a state of emergency for the zone and taking over its leadership.

However, there are still five more years left for the completion of the tenure of the elected zonal parliament. In such a case, it would not be wise to dissolve the zonal parliament with a declaration of a state of emergency. The members of the zonal parliament of the ruling party can all pitch in and help the universal president and government to solve the problems of the troubled zone. However, if the universal president believes that the problems of the zone in question have actually been created by the zonal government, and are the result of the inability, partiality, passivity, laziness, or inexperience of the zonal president and his/her government, then the universal president has the right to dissolve the zonal government, but not the zonal parliament. In this way, he/she should let the zonal parliament carry on as it is, and the universal government should assist the parliament in solving the problems.

In the event that the state of emergency is lifted from the zone, due to the resumption of law and order, peace, and harmony, and the zonal parliament has not been dissolved, the universal president can allow the zonal president and government to run the zone again until the completion of the term. But if the universal president had, under the state of emergency and due to the weakness of the zonal government, dissolved the zonal government, he/she would ask the elected members of the zonal parliament of the political party of clear-cut majority to form their zonal government again so that the newly elected zonal president and government can run the zone in a good, peaceful, creative manner.

However, if this re-elected zonal president and government allow the zone to again fall into chaos, turmoil, and violence, then this time the universal president has the right to dissolve the zonal government and parliament. If the universal president believes that with the dissolution of the zonal government and parliament he/she should also declare a state of emergency, then he/she can do so. After lifting this state of emergency, the universal president can declare a date for a general election of the zonal parliament, so that the newly elected members can form a new zonal government to rule in peace, law and order, and co-operation; the foregoing applies also in the event that there was no state of emergency declared.

Minority or coalition zonal government

If there is a minority or a coalition zonal government, and due to their inability, inexperience, weakness, and political ineptitude the zone becomes overwhelmed with chaos, with a loss of law and order, peace, unity, and harmony, then the universal president has the right to dissolve both the zonal government and the zonal parliament. The universal president should then declare a date for a zonal election after the state of emergency has been lifted and law and order have been restored.

Provincial government

The above-mentioned procedures for the declaration of a state of emergency, dissolution of the zonal parliament, and dissolution of the zonal government by the universal president and government must also be applied in the case of any of the provincial parliaments and governments.

Dissolution of the Universal Government by Non-confidence Vote

If the opposition political party or parties believe that the sovereign universal government is failing to properly conduct the affairs of the sovereign universal nation, then they can bring a vote of non-confidence in the universal parliament against the government.

Symptoms of improper conduct of affairs would be: the government has become partial and inequitable; it is misusing powers afforded it by the constitution and parliament; it is dormant and docile, indecisive and ambivalent; it does not demonstrate an understanding of the problems of the poor, the middle class, unemployed, homeless, and sick and is not doing enough to help them, its policies, planning, and actions not being creative enough to be of any use to the needy; and so on.

Prior to the motion of the non-confidence vote, the leader(s) of the opposition political party or parties must present a proposal for the vote to be signed by thirty percent of the elected members of the universal parliament of the ruling party or parties and all the opposition parties. This proposal must be given to the universal speaker of the universal parliament in the house. Once he or she has received this proposal, and it has been signed by thirty percent of all the members, then he or she must immediately bring the motion for a non-confidence vote before the house of parliament. In such a case, it is the first and foremost duty of the speaker to arrange for a secret ballot to be cast.

If the proposal is presented to the speaker at a time when the universal parliament is not sitting in the house, the speaker has the authority to call a special session of parliament as soon as possible. He or she does not need permission from the universal president or government to do this, but should inform the president and all the ministers of the impending action by any means at his or her discretion.

This special session should be attended by all members of the parliament, of all the parties (ruling and opposition), the universal president, and all of the ministers. The universal president has no authority to cancel the session; in fact, in this matter, the speaker is senior to the universal president, who must abide by his/her decision to call this special session.

For the success of a non-confidence vote against the universal government, there must be a majority of votes in favour by all the elected members of the universal parliament. If the universal president does not attend the parliamentary secret vote, for whatever reason, then his or her vote must not be counted. Once the special session is called for a non-confidence vote, it will be the duty of all members of parliament, including all the ministers, and the universal president, to attend without fail, except in the event of serious illness. Failure to attend can result in indictment and punishment. Only those who attend and who vote will have their votes counted.

If the majority of the secret vote is in favour of non-confidence, then the current universal government is automatically dissolved and the universal president dismissed. Once the motion is passed in the house, the speaker will issue a memorandum, signed by him/herself, to the president on behalf of the parliament stating that the vote has taken place and has decided in favour of dissolving the government.

In this event, the president and government are supposed to remain in operation until a new universal government is constituted. They have no right to resign, because the nation must not be left without leadership.

The dissolution of the universal government does not include the dissolution of the universal parliament. The elected members of the political party in the majority, or the political parties in coalition, can elect or select a new universal president and he or she can appoint new ministers of the universal government.

The Expulsion of the Universal President by a Non-Confidence Vote

If the universal president becomes an absolute despotic and tyrannical ruler, misusing his/her powers, and, despite a normal atmosphere, does not dissolve the universal parliament at the end of its term and set a date for a new election, and does not behave according to the principles of the universal constitution, then the leader(s) of the opposition party or parties can initiate a motion of non-confidence against the president. The procedure would be the same as that of the non-confidence vote against the government, but in this case the motion concerns the president.

Once there is a majority in favour of non-confidence, the president must immediately vacate his or her position; if this is not done, then he/she must be indicted by the universal parliament in the universal supreme court and must abide by the ruling of that court. The universal government is automatically dissolved, but will function until a new universal government is formed.

After the expulsion of the president, the speaker, on behalf of the universal parliament, must appoint the vice-president as the president of the universal nation to take over until the elected members of the ruling majority party or the ruling parties in coalition can elect a new president. The speaker, on behalf of parliament, will appoint this new leader as the universal president and this person will then form his/her new universal government.

A president who has been expelled by a non-confidence vote has no right to declare a state of emergency in any part of the universal nation, but the newly appointed or elected president can declare a state of emergency in any part of the nation according to circumstances to maintain unity and peace. Once the president is expelled, he/she has no right to introduce the motion of dissolution of parliament (the expulsion of the president does not automatically include the dissolution of parliament). However, the newly elected president, or the leader(s) of the opposition party or parties can bring forward a motion for dissolution of parliament.

If the universal president goes into hiding, due to weakness or guilt, then the motion of non-confidence against him or her can be brought in parliament in his/her absence; and if the vote is in favour of non-confidence, then he/she must be declared expelled or dismissed by the speaker on behalf of the sovereign universal government.

Non-confidence Vote against the Zonal Government

A non-confidence vote can be brought against the zonal government if the members of the zonal parliament feel this is appropriate. In such a case, the policies, planning, and actions of the zonal government are deemed not to be fruitful, the government is very dormant and docile, and has lost the confidence of its people.

The motion of non-confidence will take place in the same way as for the sovereign universal government. If the motion goes in favour of non-confidence, then the zonal government is automatically considered dissolved. (This does not imply the automatic dissolution of the zonal parliament.) The dissolved zonal government will continue to function until a new government is formed.

Non-confidence Vote against the Zonal President

The motion of a non-confidence vote can be brought against the zonal president by the opposition party or parties in the zonal parliament in the same way as it is brought in universal parliament against the universal president. If the result is in favour of non-confidence, then the zonal president and his or her government are considered dismissed. After expulsion of the zonal president, the zonal vice-president will automatically become president and will remain in office until the new zonal president is elected. He or she would be known as the "caretaker zonal president." The previous zonal government would continue to serve until the new zonal government is formed.

Non-confidence Vote against the Provincial Government

The motion for a non-confidence vote would be brought against the provincial government in the same way as it is brought against the universal government. If the motion is passed in favour of non-confidence, then the provincial government is automatically dissolved, but will continue to function until the new government has been formed. The dissolution of the provincial government does not imply the dissolution of the provincial legislature.

Non-confidence Vote against the Provincial Governor

The procedure for this would be the same as it is for a non-confidence vote against the universal president, and the motion would be initiated by the leader(s) of the opposition party or parties in the house of the provincial legislature. If the motion is passed by a majority secret vote in the legislative assembly, then the speaker of the provincial legislature will declare the expulsion of the provincial governor.

In such a case, the deputy governor will automatically take over the duties of the governor and will be known as the "caretaker governor." He or she will function in this role until a new governor is elected. The provincial government will also be considered to be dissolved, but will continue in office until a new government is formed, and is not allowed to resign until it is no longer needed.

The expulsion of the provincial governor does not imply the dissolution of the provincial legislature. The elected members of the legislature of the majority or coalition parties can elect their new leader, and the provincial speaker will appoint him or her as the new provincial governor on behalf of the provincial legislature. Then the new governor will form his or her new provincial government.

ELEVEN

THE UNIVERSAL POLITICAL PARTY
OF THE SOVEREIGN UNIVERSAL GOVERNMENT

The universal political party of the sovereign universal government is created by the universal truth and is called The Universal Supreme Congress Party. For short it can be known as the Supreme Congress or the Universal Congress. It is not based on any religion, language, race, community, society, colour, culture, area, or any nationality or economic system. It is based exclusively on universality and universalism, and its aim is to dissolve all the present nations, governments, political systems, and economic systems and to unite all the people of the world under the sovereign universal nation and government.

In this way, all the present nations of the world would be combined to form a sovereign universal nation, and their governments would be combined to form a universal sovereign government based on unity and universal sacrifice, struggle, patriotism, and firm determination of all to achieve this universal aim. All the people must join this party on all levels—individual, family, village, town, city, district, provincial, zonal, and universal.

I have written before that there would be two political parties, but in this chapter I am giving the example of one political party—the Universal Congress—to show how to create a universal nation and government.

The universal sun of the universal government is shining, but there are clouds of nationalism, politics, economics, and religionism in front of it; this is why its light does not reach all the people of the world. But the universal vigorous storm of the Universal Congress will destroy the clouds and let the people benefit from the universal sun.

The universal nation is a vast field in which the Universal Supreme Congress is sowing the seeds of peace, non-violence, unity, truth, equality, and harmony; the universal government is the fence around the field, and soon the people will reap these fruits and enjoy them.

In the beginning, there would be many governing bodies on the national level, due to the existence of so many nations, but on the creation of the universal nation, all the national governing bodies would be converted to the eleven zonal governing bodies, which would be combined to form the universal national body.

The following should be the executive members of the governing body of the Supreme Congress of the universal nation:

1. The President
2. The Vice-President
3. General Secretary
4. Secretary
5. General Manager
6. Manager
7. General Treasurer
8. Treasurer
9. General Coordinator
10. Coordinator
11. Universal Reporter

The universal reporter would give information to the governing body of the supreme congress about every part of the world and give reports to the party members from the governing body of the party.

Each of the eleven zones would have one of the above-mentioned positions, to be decided by the lottery. Suppose for the first term, the position of president went to the first zone; then for the second term it should go to another zone, and the same formula should be applied to the other positions. The distribution of the seats of the governing body would work according to the universal balance system for the Supreme Congress on the universal level, and according to the zonal and provincial balance systems for those levels.

The tenure of one term of the governing body of the Universal Supreme Congress is eight years, and one can serve only one term in the governing body of that congress in one of the above-mentioned positions. If, for example, in the first term the president is elected from Zone number two, then no candidate from the same zone can become president for the second term; for this term, the president would be elected from another zone according to the universal balance system. The length of any term can be increased or cut short in an emergency or other situation.

The tenure of one term of the governing body of the Zonal Supreme Congress is seven years, and a person is allowed to serve for only one term. The tenure of one term of the Provincial Supreme Congress is five years, and a person can serve for up to two terms. One should take guidelines from the zonal and provincial balance systems for dealing with the Supreme Zonal and Provincial Congresses.

The Universal Supreme Congress, Zonal Supreme Congress, and Provincial Supreme Congress will run the general election for the universal and zonal parliaments and the provincial legislature, respectively. All these congresses will help each other in their election campaigns.

Ex-executives of the Supreme Congress Party on all levels should always be respected and listened to by the newly elected executives, so that the party will remain united and strong. One can serve in the governing body of the party and can also serve in the governing body of the respective government. For example, one could be president of the Universal Supreme Congress Party and at the same time be universal president of the sovereign universal nation, if he or she has been elected according to the universal balance system; and so on. The same provision applies to the Zonal Supreme Congress and zonal government, and the Provincial Supreme Congress and provincial government.

The Universal Supreme Congress must be so powerful, harmonious, united, popular, creative, useful, and equitable that it should be able to support universal, zonal, and provincial governments of the universal nation, all the zones, and all the provinces. This will make the administration easier and will create universal peace, unity, law and order, solidarity, discipline, prosperity, health, literacy, and friendship in every part of the world and at all times.

All the governments should give good jobs to the executives of the Universal Supreme Congress Party at all levels so that their financial condition will remain sound, and they will be honest, busy, happy, and healthy people who will serve the people well.

All the members of all the governing bodies of all the political parties for the universal, zonal, and provincial governments must have a doctorate either in political science or economics, with five years' teaching experience and a good record. They must have all the other qualifications as needed by a member of the universal parliament. The same conditions, clauses, provisions, and methods must also be applied in the creation and execution of the Supreme Universal Unicratic Party as are applicable to the Supreme Congress Party.

All the people of all the nations of the world must join this Supreme Congress Party. All of them must parade holding the universal national flag and they must show their unity, harmony, firm determination, solidarity, and strong will for the creation of the sovereign universal nation and government. They must send their proposals for a strong government to their respective national, zonal, and provincial governments. There should be headquarters of the party in all the districts, provinces, and zones, as well as headquarters at the universal level. The personnel manning these headquarters should guide people in how to run for office and how to make this universal revolution of universal awakening successful.

Nothing positive happens without sacrifice, suffering, struggle, renunciation, unselfishness, goodwill, and firm determination. Therefore, all the people of all the nations must be ready to sacrifice their love of their nations, their desire for nationalism, socialism, capitalism, communism, democracy, religionism, monarchism, and so on. They must be ready to sacrifice their bodies, lives, dreams, and souls for the achievement of the true and real universal nation and government. For their sacrifices, this nation will repay them hundreds of times over.

All the people of all the nations must bear the word "Universalist" on their shirts. They must post the following slogans on all vehicles of all kinds, road and street signs, railway and bus stations, buildings of all kinds, libraries, temples, shopping malls, etc.

1. The Universal People and Universal Nation is the real Universal Superpower.
2. One Universal Nation; One Universal Government.
3. One Universal Nation; One Universal Family.
4. No man or woman is foreign.
5. Oneness in multiplicity.
6. The Universal People are invincible.
7. The Universal Government is inevitable.
8. The Universal Nation is inevitable.
9. Universal Revolution by the Universal Peoples.
10. The Universal Peoples are invincible revolutionaries.
11. Nationalism is evil and a sin.
12. Nationalists are failures.
13. Nationalism is war.
14. Nationalism is nuclear and chemical warfare.
15. Nationalism is debt.
16. Nationalism is poverty and sickness.
17. Awake, Universal People!
18. Universal People, unite!
19. Awaken the world.
20. One Universal Nation, one universal political system.
21. One Universal Nation, one universal economic system.
22. Struggle and sacrifice!
23. Be united! Union is strength.

24. The era of wars is over.
25. The era of Universal Peace has arrived.
26. Love begets love.
27. Forget and forgive.
28. Live and let live.
29. Where there is a will, there is a way.
30. Nothing is impossible.
31. Forgiveness is the best form of revenge.
32. Forget enmity, be friends.
33. Universal friendship is the solution of universal problems.
34. Right is might.
35. Universal Truth always shines.
36. Universal Truth is Universal Enlightenment.
37. Universal Truth is Universal Wisdom.
38. United we stand, divided we fall.
40. One world, one nation.
41. One world, one family.
42. One Universal Culture, one Universal Family.
43. Violence is cowardice.
44. Revenge is war.
45. Empire-building is militarism.
46. Universal Government is the end of all wars.
47. The Universal Nation is Universal Prosperity, Health, and Literacy.
48. Universal Struggle, Universal Sacrifice.
49. Universal Dedication, Universal Determination.
50. Universal Truth, Universal Enlightenment.
51. Universal Forgiveness, Universal Wisdom.
52. Universal Prosperity, Universal Health.
53. Universal Literacy, Universal Employment.
54. All in One and One in All.

The people should build convention halls for the Supreme Congress Party in different parts of the world, where the governing body of the party and other members can hold meetings.

I respect the United Nations Organization for all its hard work and contributions to world affairs and its honest, dedicated efforts to solve the problems of people all over the world. But the superpowers and many other nations have made it weak and it has many times failed to solve problems. Therefore, we must create an organization that is sovereign, universally liberal, solid, firm, powerful, and effective. For this purpose and for the solution of all problems, we have formed the idea to create a Universal Nation, Government, and Family; and these institutions will replace the UNO in solving every kind of problem in the world.

All the leaders of all the national governments must bring a resolution for the creation of the universal nation to the security council of the UNO. The security council must pass this resolution unanimously. After that, the UNO must declare the universal referendum for the creation of the universal nation to get the mandate of all the people. It is my firm belief that this referendum would be won with more than seventy-five percent of the votes of the people. After that, the UNO should declare an election for the creation of the universal nation and government as described in the previous chapters of this book.

An Additional Political Party for the Future

If in future the universal president and universal government believe that the two-party political system is not working for true and concrete reasons, then the president can bring a motion to create a third political party. If this motion is passed by ninety percent of all the elected members of the universal parliament, then the third party is created. The name of this third party must be the Universal Supreme Familycratic Party, which means that the universal nation, government, constitution, and peoples are of the universal family.

No one would be allowed to contest this election as an independent for any kind of government. If this third party ends up creating chaos and turmoil, then this decision can be reversed by a majority vote of sixty percent by the elected members of the universal parliament.

I have written previously about the political party in majority or political parties in minority. When political parties in minority constitute the government, then that government is known as a *coalition government*. When a political party does not have a clear-cut majority, but is in the majority among the parties in minority, then that government would be known as a *minority government*.

Now, you might say, how can there be a coalition or minority government when there are only two political parties? Here is the answer to that. Suppose two or more zones boycott the election, due to their extreme dissatisfaction with the government. In this case, it is possible that none of the parties will win a majority of candidates or seats in the parliament, and both parties end up in the minority. This would result in a *hung parliament*.

Under these circumstances, the president cannot dissolve the parliament. Both parties should form a coalition government and forget their differences, enmity, and greed for power and prestige and keep the interest of the people at heart.

The party in the majority among parties in the minority can also form a government with the consent of the other minority party or parties. But if the president believes that neither a coalition nor a minority government is working, he can go to the universal supreme court and appeal for the dissolution of the parliament; in this case, the supreme court must comply. If these kinds of circumstances occur, then any provincial governor can ask the zonal president to dissolve the legislature, and a zonal president can ask the universal president to dissolve the zonal parliament. Any provincial legislature or zonal parliament has the right to form a coalition or minority government.

I have also written about a coalition or minority government with respect to a possible three-party system in the future.

TWELVE

THE UNIVERSAL TREE OF THE
FAMILY OF WOMANKIND AND MANKIND

The universal mankind and womankind family is an ever-green, everlasting, and ever-fruitful universal tree. No one knows its beginning, centre, or end, and it is eternal. It appears and disappears from era to era, but it always continues to exist and thus never dies. Its appearance in this world brings peace, happiness, health, and prosperity; its disappearance brings disaster. Thousands of years ago, it disappeared from this planet and people suffered mightily. It has appeared again, and the era of wars and sufferings is over and the era of universal peace, health, and happiness has returned.

Universal truth is the seed of this tree, and it is its strength under which the tree stands and grows and it is the infinite space towards which the tree continues to grow forever. Mother Earth is its soil; the universal nation is its roots; the universal government is its trunk. The universal spiritual, political, social, economic, cultural, and linguistic systems are its branches, which are spreading infinitely and endlessly toward all the planets. Unity, equality, liberty, fraternity, and secularism will defend it from the autumn fog, summer heat, and winter ice of racism, discrimination, hatred, enmity, wars, and conflicts. The universal sons and daughters are the chemicals that will destroy the germs and viruses of envy.

Universal enlightenment is the sun that continues to give the light under which the tree develops and grows. Universal non-violence, tolerance, acceptance, and morality are its beautiful, charming, attractive and colourful leaves. Universal health, prosperity, literacy, co-existence, and co-operation are its fruits. Universal salvation is the nectar of these fruits.

This tree inhales the carbon dioxide of pollution and exhales the oxygen of universal clean air. Universality is the rain that showers water down to irrigate it. Universal justice is its fertilizer. Universal kindness, impartiality, knowledge, and wisdom are its fascinating and charming flowers of many different colours. For this tree, it is always spring, and so it is always bursting with beautiful leaves, flowers, and fruits. Through its branches flows the quiet, slow, scented wind.

On this tree live all kinds of beautiful birds of different colours, shapes, and sweet songs, and they are all of universal humanity. They sing the stories of the past, present, and future of this world. They are asking all the people through their songs to come to them and to sit under this wonderful, miraculous tree in the infinite shadow of universal peace, happiness, and harmony.

Celebration of the Creation of the Universal Nation

On the creation of the universal nation, by way of celebration, all kinds of student loans from universities, banks, or other financial institutions must be phased out. Similarly, all sorts of loans and mortgages on homes and farms must be phased out by all banks and other financial institutions. After phasing out the loans, they can balance their books as needed to credit their accounts.

To celebrate the forming of the universal nation, all kinds of criminals such as the criminally insane, thieves, extortionists, killers, terrorists, guerrillas, traitors, etc., must be freed from prison and must take an oath on any bible of their belief that they will commit no more crimes and do no more harm.

Unieconomy

The universal economic system is known as *Unieconomy*. Once this is established, both capitalism and socialism will become obsolete. Under this system, all people have the universal, fundamental right to operate their own private enterprise or business, and the universal, zonal, and provincial governments have the prerogative to do business as well as look after the welfare of their people.

The property of the universal nation will belong both to the people and the governments. The International Monetary Fund, the World Bank, and all other kinds of world financial institutions would operate under the aegis of the universal nation and would be known as The Universal National Bank. If private citizens have shares in these banks, then the shares belong to them.

Eighty percent of the wealth of this world is created by all kinds of workers or labourers working in all kinds of industries in the private and public sector, doing hard labour, many times ending up injured, crippled, or even dead. Twenty percent of the wealth is created by farmers working hard all year long in all kinds of weather. It is a shameful fact that many of these farmers are living under the poverty line. All the governments—universal, zonal, and provincial—must create a "Universal Welfare System for Workers and Farmers," under which these farmers and workers are awarded enough of an income each month so that they, their parents, and their families can have a good, healthy, and happy life. All the governments must share the burden of this welfare system.

There are hundreds of millions of farmers in every corner of the world who have only a few acres of land and whose only source of income is farming. It is vital that these farmers be protected and that their land remain in their hands. If this land is bought by rich people or by private-sector agricultural corporations from other provinces or zones, then millions of farmers will become landless. This will force the farmers to become slaves working for the rich landlords on their former land. Or they will become jobless and go to the cities in search of work, joining the ranks of unemployed homeless.

This situation will produce chaos and turmoil for all the governments; it can cause civil wars in the parts of the world where the land is being bought and sold instead of cultivated. It has happened in the past; it is happening now.

So to stop slavery, unemployment, civil wars, chaos, and turmoil, rich people and corporations are not permitted to go into a crowded province where farmers have small holdings for cultivation and buy land; the farmers have the right to refuse to sell. But if they want to buy land to build a home or a building for education, industry, health care, or other vital necessity, then they have a universal right to buy land. The universal and zonal governments cannot overrule the decision of the provincial government regarding land sales.

On the other hand, in those provinces that are huge in size or where farmers have thousands of acres of land, and where hundreds of thousands of acres of fertile land are lying fallow, people who wish to move to these provinces, or private sector farming corporations who wish to buy, have the right to buy this land. But it is up to the farmer to sell or not to sell.

This system is to defend millions of poor and small-scale farmers against losing their land, and thus to prevent hunger, disease, unemployment, suicide, and subjugation of the poor by the rich. But when, in the future, every part of the world is scientifically and technologically advanced, prosperous, educated, healthy, and happy, then the universal government can change this system and allow all people and private sector farming corporations to buy and sell land wherever they please, and the provincial governments will have no universal right to stop it.

Subsidies must not be given to rich farmers and private sector agricultural corporations. This is to prevent substantial drops in prices of all kinds of agricultural products, thus saving and protecting the poor farmers and defending the small-scale and middle-class farmers.

There are many areas in the world that are prone to drought and famine, due to which thousands of people and livestock suffer and die. The universal, zonal, and provincial governments must together create a Universal Drought Protection Commission and share the costs. Under the guidance of this commission, all these governments must store in advance food, water, and grass for all the people and animals of drought-prone areas. There must be an army of security forces to deliver this food and water to the people and grass to the animals if and when they are needed. They must build houses in these drought areas that can protect humans and animals from the scorching heat.

In these areas, drought-resistant trees can be planted and fitted with a special, leak-proof bucket to water them. In this way, they will stay green all the time, and animals can be fed with their leaves; the leaves will also evaporate some moisture, which will encourage rain to fall and reduce the chance of drought.

All the governments must also create universal commissions to deal with the chaos and destruction created by natural disasters such as earthquakes, hurricanes, tornadoes, etc.

Health and Prosperity Measures

All the governments must establish health care research centres in every part of the world to find cures for the different diseases prevalent in various areas, and also to find cures for chronic diseases such as cancer, AIDS, heart problems, blood pressure problems, diabetes, etc. This will increase the number of jobs in these fields. Free health care will precipitate the need for more hospitals and personnel, thus providing more jobs in the health care industry.

Giving free nutritious food to the hungry and homeless will make all the people healthy and happy, which will tremendously cut down the health care costs now borne by the government. Giving free food will increase the demand for food, so farmers will have to increase their yields and will sell more; this will mean more jobs in farming. The farm equipment industry, the fertilizer industry, and all other farming-related businesses and industries, will need more employees. All this will add to the prosperity of the farmers and those connected with farming.

Providing free housing to the homeless will cause a boom in the construction industry and will benefit all those connected with construction, such as materials, transportation of materials, and labour.

For good health one must have regular exercise; therefore, the government must open gymnasiums in every area. This will create more jobs for instructors, coaches, etc.

There must also be a government-funded space research centre. At present, the major countries of the world have space stations by the means of which they are conducting research on space technology, materials, and exploration. With the reign of the universal government, all these stations will be converted to one universal space station to perform this research, and the associated costs will decrease.

In the future, scientists will find life on other planets, and our earth will be visited by those from other planets and vice-versa. Scientists will invent vehicles that can travel near to the speed of light and will be able to reach other planets in a relatively short time. It would then be possible to transport natural resources, consumer goods, and travellers back and forth.

Thus, everyone will benefit, including the government, since there will be less unemployment, and increased payment of taxes by all the employed.

All governments should build their convention halls and rest houses near their Houses of Parliament, Legislature offices, and regional offices. Here, they can conduct their meetings and summits, and can be housed when they are in the area. No governmental leaders, ministers, officers, or executives are allowed to hold their summits, meetings, etc. at expensive hotels, motels, or resorts. As well, they are not to use expensive cars or other vehicles for travel, but must use, strong, simple, safe, economical vehicles. These leaders and their ministers and executives should be highly paid so that they cannot be bribed or corrupted.

Unisecular

Unisecular means that the universal human family, nation, and government are secular. It means the separation of religion from the governing and administration of the universal nation.

The people of the world would still be free to worship their God or gods, goddesses, saints, etc. No one has the legal right to convert anyone from his or her faith of choice by force. People of a given faith or religion have no right to condemn any faith, religion, or culture. However, a person who wants to change to a different religion of his or her own accord can do this.

Unisecular also means that all people have the universal and fundamental right to choose any political party or parties, but not in the name of any religion or culture or of any particular geographical area.

Unispirit

The universal truth is defined as the universal divine spirit, which will be known as *Unispirit*. This lives in the hearts of all the people of this world and many others. We of this world and those of other worlds are always united by the invisible thread of Unispirit. To maintain this unity and to maintain peace, non-violence, prosperity, health, and so on, and to obliterate religious racism, hatred, prejudice, and civil wars, it is vital that all people worship all the gods and goddesses.

All the Holy Scriptures teach the same central ideas, such as honesty, truth, love, compassion, non-violence, meditation, etc. Universal unity and equality exist in all of them. We do not need any kind of teacher, priest, or preacher to convey these ideas that we can read for ourselves in the Scriptures. We must keep away from superstitions and enlighten ourselves.

We must build temples where the Scriptures can be kept in honour and respect, and where we and our children can go to worship our gods and goddesses with others of all faiths. It is very true that the spiritual core of all people is one and the same everywhere, and it is known as the universal divine spirit; this spirit exists in all people, the gods, goddesses, saints, and Holy Scriptures. Multifaith must become our spiritual path; this would put a stop to religious hatred, discrimination, and wars. Multifaith would give the same spiritual identity to all people, and they would love each other and assist each other more when they know that they are all on the same path.

Anyone who preaches that one god is greater than another, or one religion is better than another, or one Holy Scripture is better than another is a great danger to world peace. This kind of thing is one of the main reasons for religious hatred, prejudice, regional conflicts, and wars. People must not listen to this.

We need both an academic and a spiritual education. Academics will be taught in all the schools at all levels; spiritual values will be taught at home and in the houses of all the gods. Different people worship the universal truth in different ways. If we read the Holy Scriptures, we find that the universal truth is in Divine Spirit, an invisible, visible, universal, androgynous Divine Being. All the different methods of worship reach the same goal and are all equal, true, and authentic.

Religious education must not be part of the curriculum of any educational institution anywhere. Students can learn about their faith and rituals at home or in the temple, church, or synagogue. These temples must be built to last and be simple, strong, and safe.

However, the government must open schools all over the world where spiritual teachers and priests can be taught to preach about all the gods, goddesses, saints, and Holy Scriptures; these schools must be financed by the governments and they must award certificates, degrees, and licences. All those who have earned a degree from one of these schools will have the right to become a spiritual leader, teacher, preacher, or priest, as well as those who have personal knowledge about all the gods, goddesses, saints, and holy scriptures.

The temples of the gods, goddesses, and saints must use the money they receive in donations from the worshippers to open food banks and small and simple hospitals in every temple. (For chronic diseases, they must go to the government-run hospitals.)

These spiritual teachers and preachers have the right to marry. They should be paid by both the government and the temple. They must not live a life of extravagance. They must always be respected and revered by the people and by the governments, and they must have all the necessities of life. These teachers would be one of the major forces to maintain the equality, unity, liberty, and oneness of all the gods and people of the world. Both males and females have the right to become priests and preachers.

The Universal Truth lives in our hearts in the form of a very tiny atom of Divine Light; this world is a microcosm and sits in our hearts in a miniature form. This world has already been united—

in our hearts. All we have to do is to wake up and look into our hearts and find it there. Then we can begin the struggle to bring this entity into external existence, with firm determination and dedication.

The Universal Truth is kind, merciful, forgiving, and a true lover of all people everywhere. It judges no one and helps all to solve their problems. It purifies sinners, evildoers, and criminals. The most heinous sinner can come into its shelter and confess his or her sin and ask for forgiveness and purification, and it will turn this devil into a saint. That is why it is worshipped by all in this world and many other worlds.

We must live the life of a saint and a warrior. As a saint, we must follow a moral, ethical, and courageous life; as a warrior, we must build a strong and healthy body by eating nutritious food, drinking lots of liquids, and exercising. We must avoid junk foods, alcohol, drugs, gambling, and pornography. As a warrior saint, we must fight with all our might against the division of this earth by uniting all peoples—by creating a universal nation.

We must live in the society of those people who are more spiritual, educated, and wise than we are. If we cannot find them, we can live among our equals and pursue spiritual studies so that eventually we can enlighten people about spiritual things. When one lamp enlightens another, then its light is increased.

Patent Rights

All past and present patent rights in the field of agriculture will become obsolete. No individual or corporation who creates a new invention or research in this field has the right to claim any patent rights. Instead, all the governments will honour these people or corporations with national, zonal, and provincial prizes and will buy the invention or research from them at a price much greater than the costs incurred. Then these governments will sell the invention to those who can manufacture it and offer new products to the economy. This is to prevent the monopoly of any one corporation and to keep the prices of agricultural products—for example, seeds—low enough for the poor and middle-class farmers. This is also applied to milk and all its by-products.

There are six billion or more people in the world, and therefore lots of markets for the private sector corporations to sell their products and produce as much as they want. As mentioned above, all kinds of agricultural products belong to all the people of the whole world, and thus to this universal nation; a farmer can sow any kind of seed or grow any kind of fruit or vegetable she or he desires.

Similarly all kinds of patent rights will be made obsolete in the field of medicine, and the process will work in the same way as that described above, so that the price of medications will remain low and affordable. The universal nation, all the zonal and provincial governments, and the supreme court of the universal nation have no right to reinstate these patent rights at any time.

Taxes and Interest Rates

We know by experience that whenever governments levy high taxes on the people and the banks increase interest rates, the economy stagnates. Recession and inflation occur, unemployment and the deficit increase, stock markets plummet, and industries declare bankruptcy. Due to this, consumer spending drops, and the demand for consumer goods decreases; this reduces the manufacturing in the industries, which becomes the cause of even more unemployment. Then, to bring the economy back on track, the government reduces taxes and interest rates, but now it is too late, because it will take years to work up to another economic boom.

A boom in the economy does not mean inflation; inflation only occurs when people have more money than available goods. In this new technologically and scientifically advanced world, with multinational corporations everywhere, there would always be more consumer goods than money to buy them, and inflation would be held in check. If inflation occurs anyway, then reduce the salaries of all highly paid persons such as judges, government officers, principals of colleges and universities, and so on, and pay it back to them when inflation has abated.

Therefore, to prevent all these economic crises, taxes and bank interest rates must always be low and reasonable. This means that people will earn more money and will buy more goods; the governments will receive more money from sales tax and a goods and services tax, and thus their revenue will increase. The increase in demand for consumer goods will result in the manufacture of more goods and therefore more jobs in the manufacturing plants. The government will benefit from this also in terms of taxes. The economy will boom in every part of the world, and people will become happy, healthy, and prosperous; the governments will become economically strong, stocks will grow, and banks will receive more money.

The sales and goods and services taxes must not be more than five percent, and the taxes on spirits—wine, beer, and liquor—must not exceed twenty-five percent. All tobacco products must not be taxed more than fifty percent. Any government to charge higher than these fixed tax amounts will be indicted and its leader sent to prison for ten years.

Those who live below the poverty line must not be required to pay income or property taxes. The income tax paid by the middle classes must not be more than ten percent, and that of the upper middle classes, the wealthy, and private enterprise of all kinds must not be more than fifteen percent. Interest rates must not go above six percent for all financial institutions, and interest on credit cards must not go above twelve percent. This Universal Tax and Interest Code must be applied all over the world equally and uniformly, and no government can change it. If change is desired, the governments have to approach the universal supreme court, which alone has the authority to do that. If such an approach is made, the supreme court must suspend all its other concerns and cases until the matter has been dealt with.

Ten percent of the total income earned by all the governments must be set aside for welfare payments to all those labourers, workers, and farmers who are living below the poverty line, whether or not they are employed. This is not showing favouritism to the farmers and labourers, because after all it has been created by their blood, sweat, and sacrifice; so the governments must deliver it proudly and happily. This tax money must be given to the supreme court of the universal nation, which body is to deliver the money to the labourers, workers, and farmers every month.

The supreme court of the universal nation can deposit this money in financial institutions and invest in the stock market, so the money for helping the needy can grow over time. The money must also be used for building homes for the homeless and to clean the slums and build homes there. All the governments must pay another ten percent of their annual income to the universal supreme court as a universal homeless fund.

The universal supreme court must charge a percentage of the annual income of all private and public enterprises to be spent on medicine for the chronically ill, first to the poor and middle class, and then to the wealthy. Here is the sliding scale of payment:

Annual net income after taxes	Pay
$10 to $20 million	1%
>$20 to $50 million	2%
>$50 to $75 million	3%
>$75 million	4%

As well, all kinds of financial institutions, including private and public sector banks, must pay three percent of their annual income to the universal supreme court as a medical allowance. Failure to do so would be considered an indictable offence with a ten-year sentence. The universal, zonal, and provincial governments have no right to interfere with the supreme court in this matter.

The universal supreme court must construct storage facilities for medications and should distribute them to the chronically ill patients in the government, Red Cross, or private hospitals (and they must make sure the patients in the private hospitals are receiving the medications free of charge).

The universal government must create a Universal Health Care Insurance Plan, which would serve all the people of the world equally. Those who can afford it would pay a health care premium every month. Others would be covered by their governments.

Stimulation of the Economy

Whenever any of the governments has a surplus of funds, it should distribute money to the poor and to the low-paid teachers, clerks, secretaries, etc. This will serve two purposes: it will help the poor, and it will stimulate the economy. All those who invest in the stock markets must pay two percent of their annual income to the supreme court of the universal nation, and this court must distribute the money to the poor so that they can fulfill the necessities of their lives and be happy. When the poor people have more money, they will buy more consumer goods, which will cause the stimulation of the economy as described above.

The decision as to who is or is not living below the poverty line or is considered middle class or wealthy, has to be made by experts in economics with a doctorate in economics from a good university and ten years of teaching experience with an excellent record. These experts must not have worked for any kind of private or public sector corporation and must not own any kind of business, nor should any of their immediate family members.

The Universal Free Trade Act/Law/Code

Under this code, there would be free trade over the whole world. People would be free to do business in any part of the world. But for a few years, until the world becomes scientifically and technologically advanced, rich, and industrialized, there will be some restrictions to prevent domination of the poor and undeveloped by the rich and advanced.

If a provincial government believes that an industry is established that is harming its home industrial manufacturing plants and thus hurting the home consumer goods market, then it can request that this new industry leave the province and find another location. However, the provincial government can do this only with the permission of the zonal government of that province.

If a zonal government believes that private sector business corporations in their zone are hurting their home private and public sector corporations, then they can respectfully ask them to leave. If a zonal government believes that consumer goods of any kind or agricultural products (including milk) are harming their home markets, then it has the right to put a stop to their importation. If any zonal government believes that consumer goods coming into its zone from other zones are cheaper than such goods manufactured at home, thus hurting home markets and manufacturing and creating unemployment and dissatisfaction, then it can set a tariff on those imports. Once the world becomes advanced and prosperous, this kind of protection will no longer be needed.

If there is a dispute between two provinces of the same or different zones, due to water or mining rights or any other such disagreement, the universal national government has full authority to combine these provinces into one and make them solve the problem quickly and permanently. If there is a small province that is crowded, then the zonal government can unite this province with its neighbouring province; in this matter the government should obtain the consent of the universal government. If there is a huge province that is difficult to govern, thus obstructing the development of the province, then the zonal government, with the consent of the universal government, can split it into two or three provinces. These decisions would be incontrovertible and could not be reversed.

The universal president and all his or her ministers, the zonal presidents and all their ministers, and the provincial governors and their ministers will have advisors to assist them. These experts will be responsible for doing planning for their departments so that matters can move along speedily. They must have doctorates with an excellent academic record and with five years' university teaching experience. These experts must not have worked for any kind of private or public sector corporation and must not own any kind of business, nor should any of their immediate family members. This is so that they will not be tempted to do favours for the wealthy and forget about the poor and middle-class people. Our goal is to make all the people in the world, poor and middle class included, prosperous, healthy, and happy, which can only happen when we have leaders and executives who are highly educated and experienced and who are aware of the sufferings of the poor and needy.

For example, a universal finance minister should be given eleven experts from each zone who have degrees in economics from some of the best universities in their area. There are eleven zones, so the total number of experts becomes 121. The eleven experts from each zone would do the planning for the development of their zone, and all 121 would do the planning for the whole world. One expert from each zone would be located in the head office of the universal president and would advise and guide him on matters of economy. Similarly, all of the zonal presidents, provincial governors, and ministers would have their experts.

Every part of this world is rich in natural resources, beauty, wisdom, wealth, literature, spirituality, intellectuals, warriors, artists, writers, musicians, doctors, and so on. Those areas that have been left behind in industry and technology were dominated, suppressed, oppressed, and robbed by foreign invaders who not only robbed them but also destroyed their infrastructure. But these scholars and warriors fought back for centuries and in the end sent the invaders back to their own homeland and kept their languages, civilizations, cultures, and holy scriptures alive. And now they are working very hard and soon they will reach a glorious golden age. They are so intelligent that with the proper education and training, in a short time their part of the world will be filled with doctors, engineers, lawyers, scientists, and technologists and their lands will become advanced and industrialized. They have wealth, but do not know where to invest it; they have natural resources, but do not currently have the technology to manufacture consumer goods.

Therefore, I suggest that they let those from the industrialized, prosperous, and advanced areas invest money in their provinces and zones, and let them open as many industries and private sector corporations as they like. This will help them to advance much more quickly. The universal nation and zonal governments must invest in these undeveloped areas, opening schools, colleges, and universities to educate the people in the arts and sciences.

The governments must open thousands of hospitals, of two kinds: one that deals with ordinary diseases and the other to deal with chronic and fatal diseases and terminally ill patients. In all these hospitals, medicine, food, rooms, and clothing must be given free of cost to all patients.

And the people on the receiving end of all this must remember to renounce prejudice, hatred, discrimination, racism, terrorism, revenge, and class struggle, or else no one will want to invest time and money in their affairs. Also, if they are involved in all that social and spiritual chaos, they will not be able to put the effort into becoming industrialized and advanced, and their development will be delayed for a long time. The governments will be unable to make them prosperous, healthy, and happy. And not only they, but their children and coming generations, will continue to suffer and struggle for nothing.

These people must live in the ocean and heaven of peace, law and order, equality, and friendship and must believe in the universal truth and oneness of all the faiths, gods, goddesses, saints, and holy scriptures. If so, then everyone will help them, and in a short time they will become literate, wealthy, industrialized, and advanced. Just consider the examples of South Korea, Taiwan, Singapore, Malaysia, Japan, and Thailand.

As all nations would be transformed into one universal nation, there would be no debtor or creditor nations left, and thus all kinds of national debt and credit would become obsolete. No zonal government would have the right to claim any kind of debt from any provincial government that was owed to the former nation that existed in that zone; the debts of all the provincial governments would become null and void. To spread wealth to every part of the world, it is vital that all the governments be free of debt.

But how would all the banks and other financial institutions recover their money? Would the whole world be plunged into a stock crash and depression? To prevent this from happening, the universal nation must allow all these institutions to balance their books, and the money they have loaned to the former nations would appear as a credit. The same would happen with the stock markets.

But moneys that have been deposited by all the national and provincial governments in all kinds of financial institutions or that have been invested in the stock market will always be available for use. This money cannot be confiscated. But the difference is this: the former nations have now become incorporated into zones, and their money will be owned by the zonal governments. All the private and public sector corporations and all the people who owe money to the financial institutions must pay that money back according to their original agreements, and the banks have to honour any deposits made. The governments have no right to impose any kind of tax on the money loaned by the financial institutions to all the nations, provinces, and municipalities.

Standard Currency

The currency of the universal nation with all its zones and provinces will be known as the Rose. Each Rose would be equal to 100 petals, just as one dollar has 100 cents. The Rose or Roses would be counted in the French decimal system, just as the dollar is counted as present. The symbol for the Rose would be an "R" with a small line crossing its centre point (₽). On any kind of bill of this Rose currency, there should be no image of any human being or of any god, goddess, holy person, etc. But there should be the image of a rose flower on it.

As the rose flower is charming, beautiful, and fascinating to everyone, so would this currency be healthy and would bring happiness and pleasure to all the people of the world. In the future, the scientists must develop a paperless universal currency.

At present, different nations have different kinds of currency with different values. Those nations whose currency has more value than others face a deficit due to the high cost of labour and thus higher prices of consumer goods. Those nations whose currency has a lesser value than others can earn a surplus due to cheap labour and the lower prices of their consumer goods. Thus, trade in this world is not fair, just, honest, and impartial. All the nations have been fighting for many years to solve this chronic problem, but they have failed.

On the creation of the universal nation, there would be only one currency, whose value would be the same everywhere, and therefore trade would always be just and impartial. There will be hundreds of millions of middle-class and wealthy people, unlimited natural resources (Mother Earth will continue to produce them as she has since the beginning), hundreds of millions in the workforce, superior technology, and an abundance of capital that will help in feeding the economy orders of magnitude better than at the present time. In twenty-five to fifty years, there would be no poor left in the world.

The Universal Hunger Fund

All those families whose personal wealth after taxes is more than thirty million dollars must pay two percent of this money annually into The Universal Hunger Fund, which will be administered by the universal supreme court. The supreme court will make arrangements for its employees to deliver food to all the hungry people so that no one will need to go without food. Anyone who attempts to avoid this tithe would be committing an indictable offence and if convicted, he or she must be sent to prison for ten years without parole and must not be pardoned. These prosperous people make their money from the hard work, blood, and sweat of the poor labourers, farmers, clerks, secretaries, etc. that work for them. Thus they must give back to society a small measure of what they have received.

Allocation of Funds for University Students

High school education—from Grade 1 to Grade 12—must be provided free of cost, shared by all governments. For the university education of all those students who are from poor families and cannot afford it, the governments must allocate ten percent of their annual income. This money is to be used to cover all costs, including room, board, and clothing. When admission is limited for any reason, then students are admitted based on merit, such as higher marks. As well, professional jobs such as managers, administrators, engineers, scientists, professors, etc., would be given based on academic standing and experience. The universal supreme court will administer these monies.

Shift Work

Evening, night, and early morning shift work in all the manufacturing industrial plants and all kinds of construction is banned by the universal nation. Any enterprise of this kind, private or public, to ignore this ban is committing an indictable offence punishable by up to ten years in prison.

Shift work can result in the wife's being at work during the day and the husband at work in the evening; or both of them are at work at the same time, and then there is no one at home to watch over the children. Either way, the children are not receiving adequate parenting, guidance, and supervision from both parents. In the absence of their parents, children end up watching movies involving drugs, violence, pornography, and crime, and they lose interest in getting an education. They can fall in with criminals and gangs and become criminals themselves or addicted to drugs or alcohol; their future would be ruined and the happiness of their parents destroyed.

People who work in the evening and late at night have no time to sleep during the night hours, which are the best for a good sleep. Working hours must not begin before eight a.m. and should finish at four p.m. The maximum overtime an employer can ask from a worker is two hours. Workers must be paid double for overtime. There must be no work on Saturday or Sunday so that the parents can have enough time to rest and spend time with their children.

If an employer needs to start up his machines before the work day begins, he can call his foremen and a few workers one hour before the shift begins; similarly, if he needs a few workers to clean up the plant, then after four-thirty p.m. he can hire a few workers to do it.

All kinds of private and public sector banks, post offices, police and security forces, prisons, transport, shopping malls, educational institutions, churches, movie theatres, hospitals, restaurants, motels, and so on can operate in the day, evening, or night—at any time they wish. The successful, prosperous, profitable, and fruitful businesses can open more industrial units to operate during the daytime and demonstrate that day workers are more efficient, healthy, and happy than those who work at night. By opening more plants, buying more equipment, and hiring more employees, the economy will improve

The Universal Welfare Fund for Women

Our mothers, sisters, daughters, etc., have been suppressed, oppressed, and depressed for thousands of years by evil and satanic forces and have suffered excruciating pain, humiliation, hatred, abuse, and death in every part of the world. They have quietly suffered all this with great patience, tolerance, and perseverance, and the Universal Truth knows this very well; this is why He and She are unequivocally going to end all this inhuman suffering once and for all by the creation of the universal nation.

Mothers bring up their children with great care, love, guidance, dedication, sacrifice, struggle, and perseverance, while having to endure hunger, hatred, abuse, and battering by their spouses and many times by their in-laws. They submit to all this torture in the belief that they have no choice and continue to love their children and raise them with great care, showing them only kindness, forgiveness, inspiration, encouragement, and safety.

In many parts of the world, women are so poor that they cannot afford child care for their children while they work; so they tie the small child to their backs by a cloth and go to work in the fields or on the roads or wherever they need to go. Many of them are so poorly fed that when they try to feed their children milk from their breasts, no milk comes, but only blood. This is the greatest injustice done to these helpless and unsupported mothers and their children on a planet where so many have so much and live so extravagantly.

These mothers are peerless in this world of hypocrisy, bigotry, deception, and manipulation. A mother is superior to a father, because of the discomfort of keeping the baby in her womb for nine months and then giving birth with such excruciating pain. Then she feeds, nurtures, and loves the baby, child, and adult that it becomes. She loves him or her honestly and unselfishly more than her life and sacrifices all for her child. All the women of this world who are our mothers have been purified by their great universal talents of patience, tolerance, endurance, forgiveness, and courage; I call them holy saints and great angels. When a mother prays for her sick children in troubled times, then her prayers pierce space in the twinkle of an eye and the crown of the Holy

Father and Holy Mother trembles in heaven, and her prayers are answered immediately.

All the people of the world must believe that they are indebted to their mothers, fathers, and teachers. At all times, in all places, and in all circumstances, they must never speak a harsh word to them, must never scream at them or call them bad names; if they do, they will lose their health, peace, respect, and good name. To pay their debt, all must honour their parents and teachers when they become old by loving, respecting, revering, and serving them. They must believe that their parents and teachers are incarnations of the Holy Father and Holy Mother.

All professional people such as presidents, kings, queens, singers, musicians, actors and actresses, etc., whose annual personal income is between one and ten million dollars must pay two percent of their income to the universal government for The Universal Welfare Fund for Women. Here is the sliding scale of payments into this fund:

Annual net income after taxes	Pay
$1 to $10 million	2%
>$10 to $30 million	5%
>$30 to $50 million	7%
>$50 million	10%

There must never be any tax on this money. The universal government must give this fund to the supreme court annually, and the court must deliver this money each month to women who need it; e.g. unemployed or those earning low wages, women whose husbands are earning low wages, battered or divorced women, single mothers, or widows with no financial support, or women whose husbands are in jail, ill, or disabled. Anyone who tries to avoid paying into this fund is committing a very serious indictable offence and if convicted must serve ten years in prison without parole regardless of position or education.

Status of Women

In this world, women are killed for honour. Under the universal criminal code, any kind of honour killing is banned. Honour killing is a serious, indictable offence and must be treated as second-degree murder.

If any man or woman commits adultery, knowingly or unknowingly, and if he and she confess it and repent and take a true oath of the Universal Truth that they will not repeat the offence, then they should be forgiven. By believing that the Universal Truth is the greatest purifier and forgiver of sins, guilt is instantly purified. If a man or woman cannot forgive adultery, then he or she can get a divorce. If they cannot divorce, then the accused can be taken to court, and if declared guilty, the court should send him or her to prison for four years.

Every woman should know how to fight for her defence and for her rights of equality, freedom, education, spirituality, and profession. She must be bold and courageous like a tiger and the goddess Kali Ma. She must keep herself physically fit by doing exercise for twenty minutes, three days a week. She must not fear her husband or any other man and she must fight back legally or physically to maintain her honour and rights; she must believe that tolerating injustice is a sin and doing injustice is a crime. If she suffers physically—even if she dies—she must believe that to sacrifice one's life, interests, and wealth to fight against injustice, inhumanity, cruelty, tyranny, suppression, oppression, etc., is always righteous. Bravery, courage, and bold sacrifice are some of the greatest forms of worshipping the Holy Father and Mother, and He and She love these kinds of great women; for them He and She will open the gates of paradise and salvation, and angels will salute them.

All women must keep a knife and a baseball bat with them at all times when they visiting or are driving a vehicle, and if they are attacked, they must use these weapons to defend themselves; they have the legal right to do so. If the offender is physically harmed or killed, then the woman must not be charged, because this is holy self-defence. Women must realize that these kinds of criminals are very cowardly people whose sins and crimes have killed their spirits, and they are always full of fear and under pressure.

When they see that a woman has weapons and will really use them, then 99.9% of them will not attack them, and crimes against women will be reduced to zero.

Let us live in the real world. Crying peace and non-violence all the time is not going to defend people against violence. Violence in self-defence is always right and legal and it is the open door for defending one's person and property and maintaining peace and law and order. By doing so sends a message to all criminals and puts fear in them so they will not think of committing any more crimes. By defending themselves, men and women will assist the governments to maintain law and order in the universal nation.

Women must always be simple, moral, ethical, respectful, sincere, and faithful. They must not wear clothing that is provocative or pornographic—tight clothing or clothing that is too revealing. It is shameless and a great sin to provoke men in this way; that is one reason they are sexually offended, kidnapped, or killed. All these women who are wearing these kinds of clothes under the umbrella of fashion and freedom are really crossing the limit of shame and disrespect and are making trouble for themselves. This is a kind of social and spiritual pollution that has contaminated the people in this world. Under the universal rigorous law, no woman on the face of this earth will be allowed to wear these kinds of clothes under any circumstances, including modelling and films. If they do so, they will be arrested by security forces and will be charged and sent to prison for at least four years without parole. Anyone who forces women to wear these kinds of useless clothes—such as in films or magazine illustrations or performances—must be charged and convicted and sent to prison for seven years without parole. And if this enemy of society is wealthy, then he or she must also be heavily fined. All women should wear a scarf at all times to cover the neck and chest; those who do not wear it will be fined one hundred dollars.

Women must earn their own respect; it is in their own hands, actions, minds, and souls. They must love and respect their husbands as an incarnation of God himself. They must not cheat him, and must love other men as their brothers, sons, or fathers.

Husband, wife, and children must keep busy reading the holy scriptures and worshipping God. This will destroy their boredom and keep the family happy and away from bad habits. They must know that the goal of life is to worship God and get salvation from heaven; not materialism, alcoholism, and drugs.

Universal Educational Institutions for Women

We know that women are sexually harassed and assaulted, chased, physically harmed, and even murdered in schools, colleges, and universities. Despite all the efforts of the governments, the people, and the police, this has not stopped; in fact, it gets worse each day. It is a great injustice for parents to send their daughters to school to study, learn, and become educated, only to find that they are not safe from harm. When a girl has been assaulted or kidnapped, their shock is limitless; the community becomes alarmed, and people become depressed, not knowing from one day to the next whether their daughters will come home from school unharmed.

There is only one solution to this problem, and that is to separate women's educational institutions from those attended by men by passing a universal education law. Up to Grade 5, girls and boys can study together; but from Grade 6 on, all the way through university, there should be institutions of learning for women only and for men only.

Women and men can work together in all kinds of offices and industries, but all heavy work should be given to men and women should be given light work. At the workplace, the women and men should talk about the gods, goddesses, and holy saints; this will purify them and give them joy, give them more physical, mental, and spiritual strength, prevent boredom, and keep them moral, holy, and ethical. They should not discuss movies or TV, which is always garbage and unacceptable and useless knowledge. At the workplace, they should keep away from pornography, drugs, alcohol, gambling, racism, prejudice, and quarrelling, and should work together like a universal family.

Education of Children

If parents want their children to become well educated, then they must teach them at home for at least an hour a day. If the parents are not educated, then they must hire a tutor to teach them at home; if the parents cannot afford this, the provincial and zonal governments together must pay for the tutor. I have seen that those children who are taught at home by their parents get top grades and become highly successful, and those children who are not taught at home are left behind. But parents must not pressure their children to get high marks—this could have a very bad effect on them. Parents must not put their own expectations on the children, such as wanting them to become doctors, lawyers, engineers, judges, etc. If the children fail to reach the goal, it could hurt them psychologically. Just teach them at home as a hobby, for fun, and make their educational foundation strong, and when they grow up they will choose a subject that interests them and will have a good career.

Parents must keep an English dictionary at home so that their children will have a strong English vocabulary. It will be easier for them when they go for a higher education. English has become a strong language in the world, and all major subjects are taught in English everywhere. Also, it is important for the children to have a broad base of knowledge that includes political science, economics, history, law, and spirituality so that they can be prepared as knowledgeable citizens and will not be fooled by politicians, economists, historians, spiritual fanatics, and especially manipulative, greedy lawyers and dishonest police. But there must be no examinations on this general knowledge material; it might create fear and pressure and prevent the students from attending the classes on it.

The Universal Social System

The universal society will be known as *Unisociety*. The universal truth, humankind family, government, nation, Unicracy, Unieconomy, Unispirit, and Unisecular are together known as Unisociety.

The social diseases that have polluted the people throughout the world, such as homosexuality, child and woman abuse, intoxication, drug addiction, gambling, pornography, prostitution, the manufacture and sale of narcotics, publication and sale of books, artwork, and movies involving sex, crime, drugs, and violence, and places of lewd dancing would be banned under the rigorous laws of the universal nation.

The manufacture and sale of beer, wine, champagne, and light alcohol will be allowed. If such were banned, many people would attempt to distill their own liquor, the impurities of which can cause severe physical damage and even death. It is my advice to all people not to drink any kind of liquor.

The universal family is founded on morality, holiness, life, and unity; social diseases ruin these universal merits, therefore the universal government will enact rigorous laws to obliterate them from the face of the earth forever. Universal freedom does not mean immorality. The woman is our mother, sister, daughter, teacher, and wife; she must be respected, loved, honoured, and defended, and to expose her body in pornographic books, movies, fashion, and art is a most heinous sin and crime. The government that allows this is the government of pimps, prostitutes, lunatics, immorality, and evil, and a constitution that allows this must be amended or it must not exist at all. No one is allowed to make a drawing, painting, or other kind of image of a naked minor; this would be an indictable offence punishable by fourteen years in prison.

Abortion

Personally, I am against abortion, because every born and unborn child has a right to live. But abortion would be allowed according to the choice of the mother, unless she has been impregnated with a female child and this is her first or second female child; in many parts of the world, people do not want female children, so there must be measures taken to protect their lives. However, if the mother's life is endangered or the pregnancy is due to rape, abortion would be allowed. Similarly, if an unmarried woman becomes pregnant due to an affair, and this pregnancy is a dishonour to her or her family or society, then abortion would be allowed.

Marriage; Common Law

If a man and woman are in love with one another and are over eighteen years of age and want to get married, then there must not be any obstacle to their marriage; however, the woman's parents must consent. No religion, culture, ethnicity, caste, etc. can be allowed to stop this marriage. A widow or widower or divorced person also has the right to remarry according to their choice. Under the Universal Common Law, any heterosexual couple over the age of eighteen has the universal right to live together as life partners, but they must register this in court, church, mosque, or temple and they must obtain the consent of the woman's parents. No person can marry or live in common law with more than one mate.

Anyone who asks for a dowry from his wife or her family is a greedy sinner and a certified criminal, regardless of his education or status. One who kills his wife because her parents did not give her enough dowry must be punished with the most severe sentence: fourteen years in prison.

Ethical, natural, and spiritual advice to young boys and girls

However, many times those who marry from true love often are not successful and create lots of family problems; often their divorce rate is very high, sometimes up to seventy-five percent. The major reason is that they do not have the consent of their parents and the blessing of their gods or goddesses, priest, rabbi, imam, etc. It does not mean that a love marriage is a curse, but the couple must try their best to get the consent of their parents, and the parents must give their consent to these kinds of couples, regardless of colour, religion, culture, etc. This will save the future of their children. Also, it will help the couple financially by reducing the cost of the wedding, and they can live with the parents until they have completed their studies and found good jobs.

If the couple gets the permission of both sets of parents, they should be married according to their religious and cultural traditions and thus receive the blessings of not only their parents but also the gods and goddesses and their church, temple, synagogue, etc.

If the couple's parents do not give permission, then they should wait until they have completed their education and have good jobs. They will then be able to afford married life and children. They could be married at a court in their area, but the court must have the permission of the woman's parents. Although the court has no right to inquire about their financial situation, it does have to make sure both lover and beloved are male and female and over eighteen years of age. After getting married, the couple still must go to the church of their choice so they will at least have the blessings of their gods and goddesses, which will help to keep their marriage happy, healthy, long-lasting, successful, and prosperous.

Divorce

Personally, I am against divorce, but I cannot be conservative about this; so divorce is allowed in the universal nation. It is allowed with the consent of both husband and wife; or with the desire of either of them, but before the court makes its decision, it must listen to both sides carefully and with impartiality and should also give particular consideration if the couple has children. If these children are older than ten years of age, then the court must listen to their problems and consider how the divorce will affect their present and future circumstances—their health, education, finances, and psychological suffering. The court should also determine whether the children are in favour of the divorce. If the divorce is going to have a very serious impact on the future of the children, then the court should not allow the divorce.

True Marriage

The relationship of husband and wife is very holy.
The marriage of the couple is Divine.
It is not unification of the bodies,
But it is the unity of two sacred souls.

The souls of the couple are two auspicious rivers.
Marriage is to mix them into the ocean of Divinity.
For a sincere wife, her husband is her everything.
For a faithful husband, his wife is his breath and step.
The fidelity between husband and wife
Is a stair to happiness, prosperity, unity,
Love, peace, and heaven.

If a husband thinks about another woman
And the wife dreams about another man,
Then both of them are creating hell
For themselves
And for their innocent children.

With sincerity, unity, promise, and dedication,
Both husband and wife do great deeds
For their pretty children, parents, and nation.

The Wife

The wife is the half of a man.
She is his bones
And the best of his friends.

With a wife, a man does mighty deeds.
With her, a man finds courage, inspiration, and help.
With her, a man finds advice, opinions, and strength.
With her, a man finds love, respect, and happiness.
With her, a man finds success, authority, and honour.

A sincere wife is a shield for a man.
An honest wife is the happiness and pride of a man.

The Husband

The husband is the true lover of his wife.
He must never be prone to alcohol, gambling, drugs, and lust.
He should always be an ideal man

For his wife and children.
He should always do his professional duties
And must take care of all their needs.

He must never think of another woman.
He must always be sincere to his wife, children, and parents
And give all of them full respect and love.
And treat his wife like a queen.
And that great home where children, parents, and wife are happy,
There the angels of heaven are always happy
And shower health, wealth, happiness, and prosperity
On all the members of that family forever.

A man must remember that his wife does not want gold and diamonds From him
But love, respect, appreciation, and honour
And if he does that, then she will never leave him
And she will certainly stand with him in happiness and suffering
And victory and defeat; good and bad.

Even a man in the grip of rage
Will never be harsh to a wife,
Remembering that on her depends
The joy of love, happiness, respect, and virtue.
The wife is an everlasting field
In which the self of man lives.

Shelters for Battered Women

The universal, zonal, and provincial governments must build houses all over the world to provide free shelter to all those women, with their children, who have been battered by their husbands or anyone else. These centres would also be available to all those women who have no place to live, and they can stay as long as they like. They must be provided with food, health care, clothing, and some money for daily necessities.

In these houses there should be small family courts to listen to the problems of the battered women and their children; those who abused them must be brought to justice and punished by the courts according to their crimes. It is the basic, fundamental, constitutional right of these women to seek this kind of assistance, and any government that refuses to grant it should resign.

The governments must endeavour to employ only females in these centres. Creating these kinds of shelters will provide job opportunities for women, and this will boost the economy of the governments, because they will get more taxes from the employed women. Providing food, clothing, and health care will boost construction, farming, medicine, and the garment industries, which again will create more jobs and more income for the governments.

Light Work for Uneducated and Unskilled Women

Various employers such as schools, accounting, insurance, and income tax businesses, banks, hospitals, airlines, the police, the military, childcare centres, and so on, must reserve light and unskilled jobs for those unemployed women who are uneducated or have no particular skills. This is to secure jobless women financially and prevent them from becoming the victims of oppression and hard labour in the industries, construction, or any other kind of manual work. It will also save them from immoral, unethical, and evil businesses, due to lack of finances. All the heads of departments must reserve jobs for these women and pay them good wages with benefits. Their working environment must be clean and healthy, and these women must be respected. Not to abide by these regulations is an indictable offence.

Shelters for Orphans

The governments must build in all areas houses where orphan children can live up to the age of eighteen years, segregated by sex. The female shelters must employ women only. These centres must also be made available to all those children whose parents are unable to provide for them due to poverty, and those who are disabled. The governments must provide these children with food, shelter, clothing, health care, education, and all other necessities of life.

The governments should build schools up to secondary education along with these shelters, and all these students must be given training or apprenticeships in plumbing, electricity, mechanics, welding, machine shop, and all kinds of vehicle body work, hobby crafts, and so on; this will benefit the students and will provide skilled workers. Those students who excel at academics must be provided with a free university education.

Population Control

Our earth has been producing natural resources abundantly since the beginning of its existence. If we were to cultivate all of our arable land, we could feed sixty billion people each year. But this does not mean we should not attempt to keep the birth rate low. The population is growing very rapidly, and to ensure health, prosperity, happiness, and education for all, it is vital to control the population size.

With DNA, fingerprint, and computer chip identification, it could be easy to keep tabs on the population. In the future, the cashless currency and electronic transfer of funds will facilitate the control of the economy.

The world is currently passing through an energy crisis. The universal nation will spend a large percentage of its income on the research of energy production by fusion. There are huge stores of geo-energy and coal energy and an infinite source of solar and wind energy.

Mercy Killing

All those who are terminally ill, crippled, or disabled, and do not wish to live any longer, can be certified by two doctors that there is no cure for them, or that their suffering is unbearable. With the consent of their family members, euthanasia can be administered by medical staff. I myself am against mercy killing, but sometimes it is the most compassionate solution.

Guns

Under the reign of the universal government, no one is allowed to keep a gun or any other kind of firearm in his or her possession, unless he or she lives in a forested area where his or her life is in danger from wild animals. In such a case it would be permitted under the supervision of the government. Also, guns can be given under licence to those people who need to defend themselves from terrorists or other criminals. Only the government has the right to manufacture firearms.

Obliteration of Threats to Society

All the people of the world must struggle to totally obliterate the above-mentioned social diseases. If you wish to live in safety and honour and do not wish for your women and children to be abused, assaulted, kidnapped, or killed, then you must revolt against these ills until they are annihilated. Do not listen to lunatics such as drug addicts and alcoholics, whether they are government officials, or highly educated, or extremely wealthy. If these diseases are not obliterated, then this society will certainly become worse than a society of animals.

All those criminals who are thieves, sex offenders, gamblers, drug dealers, extortionists, etc., and who are idle and whose only profession is crime constitute a threat to society. It would be very difficult for the government to prove them guilty in a court of law, due to the clandestine nature of their activities, and to the fact that members of society would be afraid to testify against them. These kinds of criminals should be sent to prison for up to five years without benefit of a trial.

The government should take the advice of the heads of the members of the community where these criminals live and operate; it is a natural phenomenon that people can always identify the troublemakers in a community. This may sound undemocratic, but it is to protect society and to lower the crime rate—eventually to zero. If these criminals continue to operate unscathed in society, then they will encourage the same behaviour in others; one bad apple spoils the lot. These kinds of criminals, too, must spend five years in prison.

If the heads of the communities do not want to co-operate with the government in supplying the names of local criminals, due to fear, partiality, threats, or other reasons, then the government can get a secret referendum from the people who live in the area where the criminals live or are active. If more than fifty percent of the people vote for it, then the criminals must be sent to prison. Anyone who commits a crime and who is not a professional criminal must be brought to a court of law and, if found guilty, must be punished only by the court.

The sentence for first-degree murder is fourteen years; for second-degree murder a minimum of ten years and a maximum of twelve years; and for manslaughter seven years. Once the prisoner has served the entire sentence, he/she will be released. Giving a life sentence does not bring the crime rate down.

Those who are normally law-abiding and commit a crime for the first time, due to passion, ignorance, necessity, insanity, or religion, must be treated with leniency, and the judge has the right to be compassionate and reduce the charges. Special consideration must also be given to the sufferings of the family members of the accused, especially if he or she is the sole source of support for the family. For those families, the judge must order the appropriate government to provide funds to them so that they can support themselves while the wage earner is in prison. If the social welfare minister does not follow this order made by the judge, then the judge can send the minister and his executive to prison for up to four years.

A criminal who is declared mentally ill or insane by all the physicians unanimously—doctors for the defence and doctors of the crown—must not be charged for any illegal or moral offence; he or she must be sent to a mental hospital for treatment and, once cured, should be released.

The prisons must be run and controlled by the governments; they must never come under the control of any private enterprise. All prison employees must be paid well so that they cannot be corrupted. The security services agents and all other personnel related to public security have a basic, fundamental right to self-defence. If the criminals are physically harmed in this situation, the security agents must not be charged with any kind of offence.

This world will become prosperous, healthy, educated, and happy only if the crime rate is brought down to zero everywhere. People must be able to live in peace, law and order, and fearlessness; the government's money will not be wasted on fighting crime. It is vital to obliterate all kinds of crime and criminals from the face of the earth; for that, government officials at all levels must be honest, fair, sincere, and must never give shelter to criminals for their own purposes or out of greed or fear.

Other Types of Crimes

In many parts of the world today, a wedding is an expensive affair, sometimes involving hundreds of family members, rites and rituals, feasts, and a dowry to be given by the bride's parents. This type of wedding will be banned, and any bridegroom who insists on a dowry will be arrested, along with his father, and sentenced to seven years in prison without parole. The bridegroom should bring his bride to his home and marry her with the rites and ceremonies, with friends and relatives present; but he must do the work of an honest, true, and righteous man and be his own man; otherwise all his education and status is useless and he is a greedy coward.

Sometimes it happens that a female refuses to marry someone due to her family honour or due to cultural or religious reasons, and the man in question throws acid at her. Apart from the obvious suffering and loss of beauty, sometimes the woman dies. The parents do not want to file a complaint against the man because they want to protect the honour of their daughter and family; thus the guilty go unpunished, and others are encouraged to behave in the same vile manner. This must stop.

The government must establish very efficient secret services to deal with this. When the woman is admitted to hospital, the physician or hospital administrator must immediately call the secret service, regardless of whether the victim or her family agree, and the name of the man must be discovered, either from the woman or from her family. Their names would be withheld and they would not be required to testify in court; there would be no publicity of any kind. If the woman dies, the accused must be charged with first-degree murder and if convicted must be sent to prison for fourteen years without parole. If she does not die, then he must be charged with attempted murder and if convicted be sent to prison for ten years.

Although people have the right to keep weapons such as swords, baseball bats, hockey sticks, knives (but not guns), etc., to defend themselves, if they use them offensively, they will be charged, and if convicted will be sent to prison. However, people have the right to defend themselves against thieves, extortionists, bullies, sex offenders, threat-makers, and other villains; if these kinds of criminals are harmed in self-defence, the defending person must not be charged with a crime.

Anyone under the influence of drugs or alcohol and has an accident in which someone is killed will be considered to be guilty of homicide; if convicted, he or she should be sentenced to prison for from two to five years without parole.

Any spiritual leader, priest, teacher, or preacher who sexually offends or has sex with anyone, with or without consent, is committing a serious, indictable offence punishable by twelve years in prison without parole.

In many parts of the world, people will commit homicide due to their passion for religion, culture, or honour (due to adultery), and for that they will be sentenced to seven, ten, or fourteen years in prison. Once they have finished their sentence, they are released from prison. Sometimes they are released before finishing their sentence, due to their excellent record and rehabilitation, and their repentance, showing real, honest remorse for the victim, the victim's family, and for society as a whole, and for showing respect for the law, the government employees, and the government. In other parts of the world, a person who commits an honour or religious murder is not sentenced at all. And in still other countries, a person convicted for murder, regardless of the motive, is given a long sentence, even for life, regardless of the person's culture, status, rehabilitation, attitude, state of health, and so on.

Capital Punishment

Personally, I am against capital punishment, because everyone has a right to live in safety and security. But there is a serious concern for the safety and security of society as a whole, and we cannot allow people to live in great danger due to unruly elements in our midst. It is the duty of all governments to maintain a peaceful, crime-free, prosperous, and healthy environment for all of us. Therefore, capital punishment is allowed, but only for the most heinous of crimes, such as murder, assisting terrorists in any way, assisting in an attempt to separate any area of the world from the universal nation, committing terrorism, guerrilla warfare, hostage killing, sabotage, trafficking in narcotics or sex on a large scale, and large-scale theft.

For all other crimes, no one should be sentenced to more than fourteen years, with one exception, to be discussed below; the life sentence is banned. The presiding judge should be forgiving and compassionate before sentencing a criminal to death. He should consider the criminal's education, experience, profession, service to society, social status, age, medical condition, financial condition, criminal past, reasons for committing the crime, his danger to society, and the impact of the punishment on society, his parents, wife, and children.

If the judge believes that the criminal does not deserve capital punishment, then he can commute that sentence to seventeen years in a maximum-security prison, with no possibility of parole or pardon. If a prison inmate kills a government employee or another inmate, he must not be charged with first- or second-degree murder; severe sentences to prisoners does not bring down the crime rate, and it makes already depressed inmates even more so. Therefore, this kind of crime would be considered to be manslaughter and punished accordingly.

Prison Conditions

In any prison or jail, all the convicts must be provided with good living conditions, food, clothing, shelter, and health care. There must be programs to rehabilitate them, and no corporal punishment will be allowed. There must be a big exercise yard, a library, classrooms, and church services for all faiths.

In many parts of the world, prisoners do all kinds of work in prison, such as cleaning, laundry, barbering, plumbing, electrical work, construction, sewing, making furniture, body work, finance, computer work, tutoring, etc., and they are being paid a negligible wage by the government; this is a gross injustice. In the reign of the universal government, all prisoners everywhere must be paid at the average rate for their work; if they are not, then the inmates can sue the government, and the court can order the government to pay them fairly.

No prisoner, regardless of his or her crime, can be locked up in segregation for twenty-four hours per day unless he or she requests it for protection; even in this situation, he/she must be allowed to be in the yard for an hour each morning and evening. The prisoner's open visit or trailer visit with family members must not be denied, regardless of his or her crime. However, special kinds of prisons should be built to control those prisoners where security is paramount for the government employees. Underground tunnels should be built for the movements of the employees so that they would never come into physical contact with the inmates and be harmed or held hostage.

The prisoner's family members, relatives, and friends have full rights to send food, clothing, radios, televisions, computers, money, books, and educational materials to him or her. Prisoners have the right to purchase any necessity of life from the prison store, and they can access their funds from both a savings account and a current account.

Prisoners who have special needs such as culture, food, religion, or language must be respected, and must be provided with interpreters if needed, free of cost.

If three out of four of a board of physicians—two from the prison and two from outside government hospitals—decide that the prisoner will die in six months to a year due to a chronic condition such as heart disease, cancer, AIDS, etc., then that prisoner must be released from prison. If any prisoner suffers an amputation due to diabetes, or loses his/her legs from any cause, then he or she must be released immediately, regardless of his or her crime or length of sentence.

No prisoner can be put in a double bunk in a single cell, whether in detention or in prison. It is the duty of the government to build more jails than needed, and it will create more jobs. All inhuman and dirty jails and prisons that are unfit for habitation must be demolished, and new, open, environmentally fit jails and prisons must be built outside the cities and towns so that they will not be a threat to public safety.

Many inmates are professional criminals. They must not be allowed to mix with non-professional criminals, such as those incarcerated for political crimes or crimes of passion, because the non-professionals will learn more about crime and might themselves become professional criminals when they are released from prison.

No president or governor of any government has the right to grant clemency or pardon to any prisoner. This is to prevent political favours and special favours to the rich and famous. Only the universal, zonal and provincial supreme courts have the right to grant clemency and pardon to any prisoner if the court believes he or she deserves it. Any prisoner has the right to apply, regardless of crime or sentence.

Universal Civil Code; Universal Legal Code

In every part of the universal nation, habeus corpus and due process of law must be maintained except in certain circumstances and emergencies. There must be one and only one Universal Civil Code and one Legal Code that applies to all. This is the only way to ensure peace, law and order, non-violence, equality, liberty, and unity over the whole world and for all people. These codes must be written according to the principles laid out in this book.

Convicted criminals have the universal fundamental right to appeal their convictions and apply for a pardon to the appropriate universal, zonal, or provincial supreme court. The chief justices of these courts can be forgiving in dealing with these appeals if the family of the prisoner is suffering greatly due to the imprisonment of their loved one. All cases of clemency and pardon should be finalized within six months to a year.

For all types of trials, such as criminal, civil, parole, pardon, family, etc., the government must grant legal aid to cover the entire cost of the trial to all prisoners, without any exceptions.

The universal, zonal, and provincial governments must open law schools where students can be educated to receive degrees at all levels in law, so that there will be no shortage of lawyers and judges.

Great Men, Their Crimes, and Their Rehabilitation

The history of every part of this world is full of examples in which a great man committed a crime and then repented, felt remorse for the victim, the victim's family, or even for society as a whole, and educated and rehabilitated themselves. They began to follow the ways of righteousness, morality, non-violence, and altruism.

The prophet Moses of the Jewish religion killed an officer of the pharaoh of Egypt, due to his passion for the Jews, to the gross injustice done by this king, and to the oppression and repression of the Jews by him. The pharaoh sent him to the desert, and there Moses worshipped Almighty God, Who empowered him with supernatural abilities, forgave his sin of murder, and purified him of this sin and guilt. Moses returned to Egypt and freed the Jews. Today, millions of Jews revere Moses as their prophet and teacher, and they follow his commandments with love, respect, and reverence. As well, hundreds of millions of Christians and Muslims revere him as a very holy prophet.

The Apostle Paul, according to the New Testament, was a killer, but later on renounced that sin and crime and became a devoted follower of Jesus Christ. Under Jesus' guidance and blessings, Paul became totally purified and began to spread the teachings of Jesus and to heal the sick and do many great works for the people of his time.

Maha Rishi (which means "Great Prophet")—Rishi Valmeek—robbed and killed people; but later in life, after receiving the teaching of a holy saint, he renounced his criminal existence. He began to worship the Hindu God Rama, and all his sins were washed away and he became totally purified; he received supernatural powers under which he came to know the past, present, and future. He wrote the holy scripture *The Ramayana* (which gives the biography of Rama from birth to His ascent to Heaven). He did many deeds for the welfare of the people of his country, religion, and culture.

CONCLUSION

There is one and only one thing in this world that is real, and that is constant change. Accordingly, neither is the world of yesterday the world of today, nor is today the world of tomorrow. Nature will certainly create the circumstances under which all the people of all the nations in this world will be awakened, empowered, inspired, and united to struggle and sacrifice with firm determination, hard work, commitment, and optimism for the creation of the universal nation.

Thus, we will unequivocally enter into the peerless Universal Heaven with this victorious achievement that will be the beginning of the Universal Utopia of the Golden Age. Surely all the catastrophic, disastrous, calamitous, genocidal, fatal, man-made miseries and problems will be obliterated from the earth.

If I were to make ink out of all the water in the oceans of this whole world, pens out of all the wood of all the forests of this world, and paper of the whole surface of this planet, still all of this would not be enough to write the virtues, talents, and powers of the Universal Truth. He/She has infinite numbers of planets with infinite numbers of people on them. He/She has infinite numbers of holy scriptures, gods, goddesses, angels, saints, prophets, priests, and devotees. I worship Him/Her with all the strength of my mind, body, wealth, wisdom, thoughts, and deeds. I pray that He/She will grant wisdom to all people, that they will all worship Him/Her without mundane desires, and that He/She would continue to fulfill all the wishes and needs of the people before they even ask, because He/She already knows their problems, needs, and wishes.

Faith is not enough; one must worship Him/Her and always give thanks and reverence. Then faith becomes perfect, and all will immediately reap the positive fruits of health, wealth, happiness, peace, and success.

I worship the Universal Truth and pray to Him/Her that He/She shower mercy on all people and give them the wisdom not to hate or condemn anyone, especially the poor, sick, needy, illiterate, hungry, and homeless. Anyone who condemns those who are needy will surely lose all respect, health, and wealth, and his or her prayers will be for naught. Remember that He/She hears everything without ears, speaks everywhere without tongue, sees all without eyes, creates without hands, and moves without feet. He/She can heal without fire and is present everywhere. He/She has created everything without desire or selfishness, and His/Her deeds are incredible and inexplicable.

SARVAY LOKAN SUKHNO BHAVANTU

LET ALL PEOPLE BE HEALTHY, HAPPY, AND PROSPEROUS

Appendix A

The Universal National Flag

The flag of the universal nation would have in its centre an image of the sun, which represents the universal nation and shines on this whole world equally on everyone, no matter whether they be rich or poor, wise or stupid, black or white, male or female, worker or executive. Similarly, the universal nation is like a sun that shines on all the people, no matter who or where they are.

On this flag are some other symbols: a rose, which represents non-violence, love, and peace; a book, which represents liberty and literacy; a tiger, representing courage and bravery; a balance, representing justice, forgiveness, and equality; united hands to symbolize unity and fraternity; a candle, which represents truth and secularity; an eagle, which represents solidity and strength; and a tree representing health, prosperity, and a clean environment.

Any artist can make the flag of the universal nation. According to the law, no one is to burn, tear, or destroy this flag. Anyone who does this commits an indictable offence. Everyone must honour and respect this flag.

THE UNIVERSAL NATIONAL FLAG

LIBERTY AND LITERACY

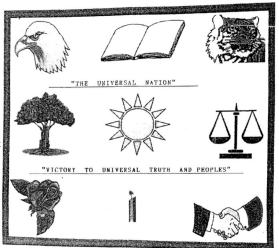

Solidity and Strength

Bravery and Courage

"THE UNIVERSAL NATION"

Health, Prosperity and Clean Environment

Forgiveness, Justice and Equality

"VICTORY TO UNIVERSAL TRUTH AND PEOPLES"

Love, Peace and Non-Violence

Unity and Fraternity

Truth and Secularity

Appendix B

The Universal National Anthem

Holy, Holy, and Holy Universal Truth,
You are Holy, Holy, and Holy.
We bow down in front of thee,
Victory, Victory, and Victory to thee.

You are Infinite, Infinite, and Infinite,
You are eternal universal divine spirit,
You are eternal universal divine Being,
You are all the gods and goddesses.
You are all the saints and holy scriptures.
You are universal, common, one and only one and the same.

You are Omnipotent, Omnipotent, and Omnipotent.
Guide us
To love and bring up our children
With care, guidance, and strength.
Teach us
To love, respect, and assist
Our spouses, parents, and grandparents.

You are Omnipresent, Omnipresent, and Omnipresent.
Lead us

To love and respect
Our universal family, nation, and government.
Bless us
To live in the heaven of
Universal unity, equality, liberty, fraternity, and secularism.
Advise us
To worship all the gods and goddesses,
All the saints and holy scriptures.

You are Omniscient, Omniscient, and Omniscient.
Enlighten us
From darkness to light,
From hatred to love,
From revenge to forgiveness,
From war to peace,
Forever, forever, and forever

You are Invincible, Invincible, and Invincible.
You are the Supreme Owner and Ruler
Of Heaven and Earth and many other worlds.
You are Creator, Feeder, and Destroyer.

You are Merciful, Forgiver, and Grantor.
Please,
Raise our universal nation
With pride, grace, and dignity.
Raise our universal flag
High, higher, and highest
With glory, honour, and fame.
Protect our universal nation
From present and future dangers
And keep it alive, alive, and alive
Forever, forever, and forever.

Holy, Holy, and Holy Universal Truth,
You are Holy, Holy, and Holy.
We bow down in front of Thee.
Victory, Victory, and Victory to Thee.

Appendix C

The Universal Manifesto

"WHERE THERE IS THE INVINCIBLE UNIVERSAL TRUTH; WHERE THERE IS HIS INVINCIBLE UNIVERSAL BLESSING; WHERE THERE IS HIS INVINCIBLE UNIVERSAL WILL; WHERE THERE IS THE INVINCIBLE UNIVERSAL FAMILY; WHERE THERE ARE THE INVINCIBLE UNIVERSAL PEOPLE; WHERE THERE IS INVINCIBLE UNIVERSAL UNITY; WHERE THERE IS INVINCIBLE UNIVERSAL EQUALITY; WHERE THERE IS INVINCIBLE UNIVERSAL LIBERTY; AND WHERE THERE IS THE INVINCIBLE UNIVERSAL FRATERNITY, THERE IS ALWAYS AND CERTAIN UNIVERSAL GLORIOUS VICTORY OF THE INEVITABLE UNIVERSAL NATION, WHICH WILL BE THE UNIVERSAL MOTHER OF THE UNIVERSAL UTOPIA OF THE UNIVERSAL GOLDEN AGE."

ABOUT THE AUTHOR

PHOTO

Dr. Pundit Kamal is the ex-principal of the S.B. College, New Colony Palwal, in India. He founded this educational institution in 1972 and administered it until 1981. He arrived in Canada as a landed immigrant in June 1981. Originally, he is of village and post office Bassi-Kalan; Hoshiarpur; Punjab, India.

The author has a university degree from Agra University, India, in political science, sociology, English literature, and Hindi. He has an honorary doctorate in divinity.

Dr. Pundit Kamal is certain that the creation of the Universal Nation is inevitable. He sees coming generations living in a utopia of everlasting springtime, in a state of peace, health, prosperity, and a clean environment.